THE LAWYER

BLOOD
MOON

as written by
ERIC BEETNER

AN EDWARD A. GRAINGER SERIES

ISBN: 978-1-943035-24-3

www.beattoapulp.com

CONTENTS

CHAPTER ONE

As The Lawyer watched the plume of thick, dark smoke curtain the sky to make midnight out of daytime, the death wagon appeared coming over a rise in the trail. The driver wore black and hung his head low as he urged his horse, a shade darker than the smoke in the distance, up the dusty path.

The Lawyer guided his stout and loyal mare, Redemption, to the side so the wagon could pass. He tipped his hat and the undertaker, who wore no hat at all but probably should have. The man's hair stuck to his scalp like the pelt of a dead skunk covered in lamp oil. The undertaker dipped his stubbly chin low in acknowledgement. The wagon wheels squealed in protest at the incline and reminded The Lawyer of an animal caught in a trap.

There were two bodies stretched out on the wagon bed. Uncovered. Both men, in their twenties and that's where the counting would stop. Bloody shirts had dried stiff to their chests, and no boots. The Lawyer knew this meant whoever had killed them was no good. Kill a man in self-defense and you let him lie, but kill a man out of spite or hate or pure meanness and those were the kind of fellas who'd steal your boots. It could be the clue he'd been looking for.

"Afternoon," The Lawyer said, easing Redemption to a stop, and the wagon slowed too.

"Most folks be riding away from a fire like that," the undertaker said.

The Lawyer looked up again at the horizon and the forest fire burning there. It spanned nearly to the edges of what he could see. Still a few miles off, though.

"I've been seeing that smoke for a few hours now."

"Been burning three days."

"Reckon that's not what did in these poor gents, though, is it?"

The undertaker smiled yellow teeth. "Not these 'uns. Killed dead in the street. No one found 'em 'til morning. Now I'm takin' 'em out where the unnamed go to rest."

Without a box to lie in, The Lawyer noted to himself.

"Has the man who did it been caught?"

"Nope. All was said and done by the time the rooster crowed. Whatever beef these fellas had, got settled at the end of a knife and that's all she wrote."

The Lawyer looked over the bodies and counted the knife wounds—three to a man. "You got much for law in your town?"

The undertaker gave him a crooked look. "Much as we need." He eyed the Lawyer's stovepipe hat. "You got much for hat makers where you come from?"

"Much as I need, I guess." He tipped his brim and gave Redemption the slightest of heel to the ribs and they were moving again.

"Hey," the undertaker called. "I could use a hand getting these boys planted. Pays fifty cents a grave. We don't even have to sink 'em too deep. Ain't nobody gonna come lookin' fer them."

"Thanks anyway, friend. I have business to attend."

The undertaker turned in his seat and called out to The Lawyer's back. "I could go seventy-five cents. You'd have to do most of the diggin' though."

"Thanks just the same. Any luck, I'll be sending more business your way."

With a wave of his hand The Lawyer dipped below the rise he'd seen the wagon climb earlier.

* * *

He watched the smoke move with the wind. From so far away, without the threat to his home or his body, he found a beauty in the fire. Now and then he could see a faint orange glow of flame at the bottom edge of the black, but it was mostly smoke rising and curling into shapes and then spreading wide to darken the sky with haze like thick butter on burnt toast.

He couldn't help thinking how those two men in the death wagon may have been the handiwork of Big Jim Kimbrough, the man he was hunting.

Kimbrough had made a narrow escape outside the town of Sundown where The Lawyer got delayed. He'd been tracking him east ever since and never felt so close as he did now seeing those flames miles ahead—he could smell the stink of him like ash in the air.

It was the best lead he had right then on any of the men who took his life away. He could still walk and ride, talk when he had to. He could still do the job of Lawyer if called to it, but his life as he knew it died that night along with his wife and children. And Kimbrough was among the gang who did it. For that, Kimbrough would die. Not out of spite or meanness, but for justice. He could keep his damn boots.

* * *

Up ahead a rider waited. The Lawyer saw him upend a canteen and then bring it down, frustrated. He approached slowly, reining in Redemption and brushing back his coat so his revolver was only a finger's touch away.

"I seen you coming," the rider said. He was a skinny man, his shirt dirty from the trail. He carried a sleep pack, heavy saddlebags, a Remington. Fit for a long journey. The Lawyer noticed a second pair of boots tucked in under his bedroll.

"I seen you waiting," The Lawyer said.

The rider held up his canteen, tipped it over to show it was empty. "You got any water?"

"I might spare a bit."

He never took his eyes off the rider as he reached behind him and unstrapped his canteen. He did it with his left hand, keeping his right free for a quick draw if needed. The rider watched him with thirsty lips. When The Lawyer tossed him the canteen he drank deep and let out a satisfied sigh of relief when he came up for air. While the man's head was tilted back in drink, The Lawyer took the chance to look around the area for other riders, maybe some with guns and big ideas. He saw nothing.

"Much obliged, mister." The rider wiped his mouth with his sleeve. "What are you out here all by your lonesome for?"

"I could ask you the same."

"Me? I'm looking for work if you got any. Been a stretch since I ate regular."

"I don't have any work for you. Grave digger up the trail a piece was offering seventy-five cents per grave and he was toting two bodies with him. You could catch him if you ride hard."

The rider took another sip of water. "My back don't agree too much with digging."

"Man looking for work ought to have a strong back."

"Maybe that's why I been out of it for so damn long." The rider laughed at himself.

The Lawyer held out his hand to ask for his canteen back. The rider tossed it to him.

"So, you out looking for work too, mister?"

The Lawyer shook his head. "I'm looking for a man."

"What man?"

The Lawyer glanced around again. Nothing to see.

"A man named Kimbrough. Big Jim Kimbrough."

"You don't think that's me, do you? My name's Lewis. What are you, some kind of law man?"

"Some kind."

Lewis shifted in his saddle. "What d'you want with this man Kimbrough?"

"That's my business."

Lewis scratched at his beard, looked out over the horizon. "Nasty fire out there."

"It'll burn out soon."

"You say so."

The Lawyer's steady gaze seemed to unnerve Lewis. He reined his horse around in the other direction. "Thanks again for the water." Lewis kicked his heels and the horse took off at a run. The Lawyer watched him go, wondering about that second pair of boots.

CHAPTER TWO

The trail took a turn to the right. Through a break in the trees on the left The Lawyer could see a wide valley and a river running at the far edge. The plume of black smoke hovered over the hills on the far side reminding him of his own tall hat. He smiled to himself.

The first bullet tore the smile from his face.

His head jerked back, the very hat in his thoughts a moment ago was now tumbling through the air, two holes marking the bullet's path. The Lawyer felt the world tilt, a pain invaded his skull and he was falling. No control over his arms or legs.

Two more shots ripped bark from surrounding trees and Redemption, with The Lawyer out of the saddle and on his way to the ground, bolted forward and ran along the trail.

The Lawyer landed flat on his back and his wind left him. His head swam with murky water. The black cloud overhead could have been the fire or it could have been his own eyes drifting shut for the last time. He tried to roll onto his side but his body would only wobble in place. He might as well have been hog tied.

A fierce pain lit across the top of his skull like a razor cut doused in alcohol.

Riders approached. Two, maybe three. More?

"Told you I got 'im," said an eager voice. Something about it The Lawyer recognized.

"I got him," a second more authoritative voice corrected.

"Bullshit."

The sound of a Remington loading another bullet.

"All right, all right. You got 'im. Either way, he's got but good."

The Lawyer felt the blood run hot on his face. His limited vision went red from blood pooling in his eyes. His ears filled with it, it ran down his chest. The right side of his head felt hot. He still wasn't thinking straight. All he could do was lay there and listen.

"This the feller?" the stern voice asked.

"Yeah, that's him. Said he was looking fer ya, Jim."

So it was Kimbrough. And the other voice he recognized—Lewis.

"Well, I guess I found him first." Kimbrough laughed and the other voices laughed with him. The Lawyer thought he could pick out three more men. He lay still, his head wound going from hot to cold now as the air hit what he knew to be open skin.

"That's a lotta blood," said a new voice. "How many times you hit him?"

"Yeah, Jim, maybe we both got 'im."

"Only thing matters is that he's got."

The Lawyer tried to focus on the figures crowded over him. They ringed him in a horseshoe, all looking down like he was something they dropped. Kimbrough leaned forward. It was the first time The Lawyer was seeing him in the flesh, but he'd memorized the photo he saw in the Abilene sheriff's office. Kimbrough looked slightly meaner in real life. His ears hung low, his face seemed stretched out like taffy pulled in a hot sun. His lips were thick and his eyebrows dark and bushy over narrow eyes.

"Knew you right off from that stupid fuckin' hat, partner."

Another round of laughs from his pack of hyenas.

"Guess you won't be tracking me no more. Cain't say as I'll miss you."

Kimbrough spit but The Lawyer didn't feel it hit him. His body was focused elsewhere.

"Aw, hell, Jim, he's already dead."

"Will be soon, I reckon."

"Naw, lookit him. He ain't moved."

The Lawyer held his breath.

"Well," Kimbrough said as he reared up on his horse. "Bury him, Lewis."

Kimbrough's horse turned away and two others followed. Lewis wasn't happy about the assignment.

"Why me? I told you, Big Jim, I got a bad back. I can't be digging no grave."

Kimbrough's voice was already far away. "Best make it a shallow one, then." The laughter of Big Jim and his boys trailed off.

Lewis, now alone with what he thought was the corpse of The Lawyer, slapped his hat across his thigh. "Shit."

The Lawyer watched through slit eyes as Lewis climbed down off his horse and took a quick look around for a place to bury the body. The Lawyer heard the man's boots crunch through the gravel near him and step off the trail a bit. He knew if he could get to his six shooter he'd have a chance to kill Lewis before he was buried alive. His arm wouldn't cooperate, though.

He felt trapped under ten feet of mud. He managed to turn his head and saw Lewis's boots stop and turn back for the trail. He also saw his own gun, thrown clear of his holster and nestled against a fallen branch six feet away. Too far to get to if his body wouldn't allow for a six inch move of his own limbs.

"Why you son of a bitch, you ain't dead at all."

The Lawyer looked up at Lewis standing over him grinning. "Bet you didn't think you'd be seeing me again, did ya?" He smiled like he was posing for a portrait.

Lewis reached down and turned The Lawyer's head by pushing on his chin. He whistled high. "Shot right in the damn head. I still say it was my shot what done it. Fuck what Big Jim says." He shoved The Lawyer's jaw as he let go. A live bolt of pain shot through The Lawyer making pin pricks along his arms and legs.

"Now then," Lewis said, "let's see about those boots you got on."

The Lawyer felt tugging on his left boot. He focused all his strength on that foot and kicked. He jerked the boot out of Lewis's hand, bumping his chin as he did. Lewis stumbled and made a move for his gun when they both heard the rattler.

Lewis shuffled back, kicking up dirt. A diamond-back was coiled in a dead log next to The Lawyer's leg. He seemed to have had enough of the disturbance to his nap and now he shook his angry rattle at the men to make them clear out—if only The Lawyer could. The Lawyer's boot hung off his foot, only covering his toes.

"Jesus, Mary and Joseph. That sumbitch was sittin' there the whole time."

Lewis did an adrenaline fueled dance and shook out his jangled nerves as he edged a better distance from the snake.

"Could've got me if I weren't lucky."

The Lawyer thought the words, *Your luck's run out if I can reach my gun.* Then he found that he'd said the words out loud.

Lewis laughed. "Well, friend, I'd sure like to see you try." He got a sparkle in his eye and picked up a fallen pinecone. He threw it at the snake who resumed his rattling. Lewis picked up another and tossed it dead on so it bounced off the diamondback's triangular head. The snake shot forward and bit down.

The Lawyer cried out as he felt the fangs sink into his exposed calf. Lewis let out a hoot like he'd won a prize at a carnival with his marksmanship.

The snake released then slid its long body under the log and out of sight, rattle sounding the whole way and sticking up behind him like a middle finger.

"Well, damn, son—you snake bit now."

Lewis seemed to think it was hilarious.

"Saved me a whole lot of digging too. I ain't gonna bust up my back planting you. I'm gonna set me a race as to which takes you first, the shot to the head or the snake bite. Either way, y'all can keep your boots. Too small for me."

The Lawyer swore he could feel his leg begin to swell. He felt the venom under his skin, felt his muscle stiffen.

Lewis climbed atop his horse. "Maybe next time you won't go giving strangers your canteen. Oh wait, there won't be no next time."

With a laugh as mean as the snake's rattle, he rode off and left The Lawyer to die.

CHAPTER THREE

A familiar exhale woke him. He lifted one eyelid and saw the dark shape of a horse's muzzle over him, felt the warm breath of Redemption on his cheek. His body wouldn't move for him. The horse nudged his shoulder and it sent a shockwave of pain through his veins. He groaned low and the horse responded with a whinny.

The sharp rattle of the diamondback sounded again. The Lawyer twitched, his limbs all responding finally, but only in reflex to the sound. He managed a half roll to the side away from the snake.

Redemption huffed and snorted a mixture of fear and anger. Then, like she had vengeance in her heart, Redemption reared up and came down with her front hooves on the snake. The rattle silenced. Redemption stomped twice more on the snake, turning it to pulp under her heavy shoes. The lawyer faded again.

* * *

He felt a presence. Hands. An ear bent close to his mouth to check for breathing. Then a tightening strap around his leg. He tried to open his eyes, but the world was a blur. Vague shapes passed before him, but no one spoke. He felt his body lift at the shoulders. Pain lit through him and the world went black again.

* * *

The Lawyer awoke in bed.

He shifted. His leg felt as if it has been run over by a wagon wheel. His skull throbbed. He reached a hand to touch it, grateful that he arms were moving again. He felt a thick bandage there.

"Easy now." A woman's voice, quiet in the dim room.

He tried to make a sound but his throat felt packed with dust. He coughed and the rattle of his bones made his whole body ache.

"Where am I?"

"Safe," she said.

He turned to the voice and saw a woman sitting with knitting in her lap. She reminded him of a schoolmarm. A simple, unpainted woman with her hair in a bun, a brown dress a size too large and a serious look on her face that emphasized the creases there.

"My horse?"

"In the stable," she said. "Wouldn't leave your side for a second."

"I was shot," he said.

"And snake bit. We didn't think you'd make it to morning."

The Lawyer turned his head to the window. Beyond the pulled curtain he could see dawn light. He looked down at his leg. It too was bandaged.

"You a nurse?" he asked.

The woman set down her knitting. "No. But Belle can sew anything and she took care of you just fine." She stood and called out the open door into the house. "He's awake."

Two more women appeared at the doorway—one a teenager and one much older.

"This here is Belle," she gestured to the old woman. "And this is Susanna." She pointed to the younger who curtsied. "And my name is Ruth."

The Lawyer nodded. "Smith," he said, using the fake name he traveled and hunted under. "J.D. Smith."

"Well, we have some questions for you, Mr. Smith. How come it was you came to be shot up there on the trail?"

The Lawyer winced as he shifted his body. "I was ambushed."

"Do we have any reason to fear you?"

The state he was in a prairie dog had no reason to fear him. He shook his head anyway to reassure her.

Ruth folder her arms across her flat chest. "Because we don't take any guff. You might see three women but we run this whole place on our own and we all three know how to use a gun."

"And knitting needles," The Lawyer said.

Ruth hesitated. She wasn't sure if he was making a joke. Susanna giggled behind her.

"Anyway," Ruth said. "Seems like we got the poison out before it spread too far. You might not lose that leg, but time will tell. You won't die anyway."

"I'm in your debt."

"You're lucky I was out and heard the shots. I must have made it to you only minutes after you were bit."

Susanna stepped forward. "Your horse killed the snake." She blushed red, as if speaking out loud to a strange man was against some list of rules.

"Redemption," The Lawyer said.

"You could call it that," Belle said.

"My horse's name is Redemption."

The three women nodded with understanding.

"Let's see if you can keep down any broth," Ruth said.

* * *

He ate a cup of clear broth and a hunk of bread while sitting up in bed. The three women stood and watched him intently. They were a mixture of Belle's hardness, Ruth's wary concern and Susanna's childlike curiosity.

"I was shot in the head," he said. "How am I not dead?"

"It cut a gash in your scalp," Ruth said. "Clear to the bone, but didn't go in."

"Lotta blood," Belle said. "But I saw many worse during the war. Stitched you up good and tight. Won't even notice it when you comb your hair."

"And the snake bite?" he asked.

"We know how to handle those around here," Ruth said.

The Lawyer dabbed at his mouth with a napkin. "As I said, I'm in your debt."

"That's not necessary."

"Doesn't change the way I feel about it."

Susanna came and cleared away his bowl. She was pretty, he guessed eighteen. Skittish like a mouse. He noticed all three women wore dresses made from the same fabric.

"Mind if I ask where all your menfolk are?"

"Dead, if you must know," Ruth said. "After my Clint passed on—the scarlet fever got him two years ago—I asked Belle to move in with me."

Belle took over her story. "I lost my husband and both my boys in the war between the states. Senseless thing. I patched up two to three hundred boys and saw them go back to war. Watched more than three dozen come back dead. Made me wonder why I did it."

She was sour, but with good reason, thought The Lawyer. Strong, and a hard-earned strength.

Susanna took a step forward as if she were reciting in a classroom. "My daddy and momma were both killed when our wagon went over a ridge. I was twelve then. I'm eighteen now," she said with pride.

"So there you have it, Mr. Smith," Ruth said. "Maybe you can tell us some about how you came to be out on that trail."

"Don't get many new stories around here," Belle said. "And I'm sick of all hers." She crooked a thumb at Ruth who shook her head at the playful ribbing.

"And we only have three books," Susanna said. "One of them is the Bible so that don't count."

"Doesn't count," Ruth corrected.

He was not eager to tell his story. "Perhaps I should rest a while."

Ruth gave him a crooked eye. "Perhaps."

"You ladies are kind."

The three women moved through the door. Ruth spoke over her shoulder. "Just keep in mind we aren't your nursemaids and we aren't your mommas. Soon as you're able, you get your own drinks and maybe work off some of that kindness in the fields."

"If the fires don't work this way," Susanna said.

"Wind's blowing east," Belle said. "Besides, they'll burn out before they ever make it this far."

The Lawyer put his head back on the soft pillow. He debated whether he should tell them the truth about his past. Would they kick him out if they knew he planned to kill some men? He wasn't sure, and he wasn't thinking straight just yet.

Through the window he could see a hazy glow of the full moon, obscured by clouds of smoke. They turned the moon a dark orange, verging on red. A blood moon, so he'd heard it called before. By his grandmother as he recollected. According it her, it meant bad things were coming.

CHAPTER FOUR

Lewis found Kimbrough at the saloon. It wasn't a long search.

Lewis had taken his time, stopping off for a shave and a haircut, then a roast beef sandwich on stale bread. His pocket still jingled with the coins they took off the two boys they'd shot out back of the cathouse two nights ago. He was hoping to sell that extra pair of boots for a dollar or two as well.

He thought about buying a new hat after his haircut, but some things a man just grows used to. Sweat-stained and sun bleached, his old hat rode comfortable on his new two-bit hairdo as he stepped into the saloon.

Kimbrough had a woman on his lap at a table in the far back corner. Big Jim was always good about staying inconspicuous. All that time on the run had gotten him spooked about making a spectacle. Too many men on the run from the law or some crackpot like that lawyer had gotten themselves found out by drinking too much liquor or raising too much hell.

Creole and Spike were with him, but their laps were empty. The two skinny cowhands had been with them like a pair of saddlebags for more than five hundred miles on this jaunt. They'd joined up outside of Texas and Lewis couldn't quite remember how they'd gotten there. They just seemed to arrive on the trail behind him and Kimbrough, and Big Jim let them keep on. They were quiet boys anyway, and both could shoot the tail off a rat at fifty paces. Nobody seemed interested in contesting Lewis for the job of Kimbrough's second man. They saw how much crap was hoisted on Lewis daily and rightly stayed to their jobs as riders and hired guns.

Lewis spotted the bottle on Kimbrough's table and stopped by the bar for a glass on his way back.

"Lewis," Kimbrough announced. "Back from the dusty trail."

Spike, dark haired and sunken-eyed, saw his face and said, "All prettied up too. Like it was Sunday and he was going to hear the preacher." Creole stayed quiet with a smile on his face that showed his rotten teeth. His clay-red skin made him look angry all the time and those teeth kept him in such constant pain he was always one short step away from bursting into violence.

"Yeah, boy, you look pretty as a picture. I declare." Kimbrough saw the empty glass in his hand. "Sit on down, son. Pour one."

"Thanks, Big Jim."

"Not at all, not at all." He patted the whore's thigh, and there was quite a lot of padding to touch. "Least I can do for a man who's been doing all that digging."

The boys chuckled.

"You boys out mining or something?" the woman asked. "Not much of it around here."

"Planting, ma'am," Kimbrough said with a smile. "Planting."

"Oh, you boys farmers?"

They all laughed at that.

Lewis knocked back his drink. "You know, Jim, I didn't even need to get myself dirty with that mess. Saved my back from pains, too."

Kimbrough's smile dissipated like the smoke from a blown out candle. "What d'you mean?"

"Well …" Lewis looked at the woman, not wanting to confess to anything with her around.

"Beat it, honey." Kimbrough bucked his leg and she bounced off like a rodeo rider.

"But you said we was gonna—"

"I paid you for your time. Go wait in the corner. I said scram."

The big gal reluctantly went, not too surprised a customer would treat her like a beast of burden.

Kimbrough lowered his voice and stared at Lewis. "Now say your piece, Lewis."

"He was dead, is all. Well, gonna be anyhow."

"What do you mean, *gonna be*?"

"He was shot in the head, Jim. Plus, he was snake bit. Big ole diamondback. Was sitting there the whole time. Why it would've bit me if I—"

"You mean he wasn't dead when you left him?"

"Not all the way, but he was headed there sure as the sun goes down at night."

"You idjit."

Lewis reached to pour himself another drink. Kimbrough snatched the bottle away.

"A man don't drink unless he does a job proper."

"To what end, though? Someone comes across him, they'll see he was snake bit and nobody will be lookin' for us. Not unless one of you boys suddenly grew fangs."

"What about the shot wound?"

"A gash on his head was all. Mighta come from falling off his horse, or falling to the ground after the snake got him. Trust me, Jim, he's dead and not about to go telling any tales.

Kimbrough cradled the bottle in his hands. "I don't doubt he is. You didn't do the job proper is all. Leaves me with a worry and here I was just getting to thinking about things without a worry for the first time in a long time. I was starting to think what I was gonna do without that fool lawyer on my ass day and night. Started feeling like a noose was being untied from around my neck and then here you come and tell me I got a knot in the rope."

Lewis held his hands up, pleading. "You don't gotta worry, Big Jim. He's dead. Dead as a door nail, I promise. You saw the blood. And the snake, why if you coulda seen the snake."

Kimbrough held a sour face, his whiskers and trail dust a sharp contrast to Lewis's freshly scrubbed skin. "What say at first light you ride back out there and make sure. What say you bring me his ear for proof. You can carry it in that dumb hat of his."

"I'll do that, Jim. First light. I'll do it, I swear."

The whore made her way back to the table, petticoats rustling like fall leaves.

"Hey there, Romeo. I got another customer so if you and me ain't gonna—"

Fast as that snake had struck, Lewis watched Kimbrough whip out his eight-inch Bowie knife and slash the whore across her cheek. Lewis felt the sting of the cut, knowing it was Big Jim's frustration with him that made him lash out at the poor woman.

She screamed and tumbled back over a chair. Creole and Spike were up out of their seats, hands on guns just in case. The only three other men in the saloon froze to the spot. No one, it seemed, wanted to be a hero on the whore's behalf, even her new customer stood rigid against the bar.

The bartender waited and saw nobody was going to do anything about the attack. He sighed once and then yelled, "No call for that in here. You boys get on out now."

Kimbrough turned to him with hate in his eyes. Something about the fresh blood in the air seemed to take him to a dark place.

"Daisy, you all right?" the bartender asked, though he didn't come out from behind the safety of the bar.

Daisy whimpered from the floor where she lay in a heap with both hands clasped over her cheek.

"She interrupted me after I told her to wait," Kimbrough explained.

"I think you'd best go on and leave, mister," the bartender said. "Looks like Daisy might need the Doc. Percy, could you—"

The man closest to the door didn't even wait for the full request before he dashed out and left the knife-wielding stranger behind. Kimbrough looked down and saw the still-bloody knife in his hand.

"No man tells me where to go."

"This is my place and I got a right to ask you to leave." The bartender's hands disappeared behind the bar. Every man in the place knew he had a gun stashed there.

Creole and Spike stepped forward, their revolvers trained on the barman. Lewis took the chance with all the men's backs turned to pour out another shot of whiskey and down it quick.

Kimbrough walked across the sawdust floor to the bar. Nobody else moved. The room looked to be full of statues. Even the barman kept his hands below the bar, his eyes unsure if he could outdraw the two skinny trail hands approaching him.

Kimbrough bellied up to the rail. The barman swallowed hard. It looked to Lewis like he'd tried to down a boiled egg in one swallow. The place wasn't fancy, but it made an attempt. The barman wore sleeve garters, a cravat at his neck, a thin mustache that curled up at both ends and hair pasted down with enough pomade to grease a pig at the county fair.

Big Jim held the knife up between them. Daisy's blood dripped down the keen edge of the blade. Without a word he reached for the barman's cravat and pulled it loose from his shirt collar. He jerked forward and the barman bent, his hands coming up empty to brace himself against the bar. Kimbrough brought the knife down and spiked the purple silk of the cravat to the bar top. Lewis could see sweat dripping off the barman's forehead.

Kimbrough reached over the bar, took a full bottle of whiskey, and leaned back. He got his face right up close to the barman.

"Nobody tells me where I can and can't go. Nobody."

Daisy let out a whine from the floor. Kimbrough gave a look her way. "You tell the doc I'll pay for any sewing he has to do on her. Don't nobody let it be said I don't pay for my mistakes."

With a smile he lifted the stolen bottle in one hand and yanked the knife out of the bar wood with the other. He tipped his hat with the hand holding the bloody knife and led the gang of outlaws out the door.

CHAPTER FIVE

The sound of shutters banging open entered The Lawyer's dream as gunshots and he jerked awake.

His surroundings were unfamiliar, pain flared from his leg and his scalp.

"He's still alive," Belle said as she looked in through the now open window. Scrutinizing him, she worked her chin until it was halfway across her face and looked out of joint. "Barely," she added.

Ruth appeared in his doorway and The Lawyer remembered.

"Morning, Mr. Smith." Ruth entered the room with the determination and energy of a bronco. "We talked about it last night after you drifted off." She scoffed. "Passed out was more like it." She set a palm on his forehead, paused to feel the heat. "Decided that if you made it through the night you might be worth a little more of a formal looking after so we're going to send Susanna to town for some medicine. Whatever the doc recommends."

She stood and clapped her hands once. "We got breakfast. Think you can walk?"

"I'll try."

"Good. That leg is still swollen up pretty bad. And it's gone a shade of purple I haven't seen since the curtains in the parlor at my husband's funeral. But if you think you can make it …"

She stood back and waited for The Lawyer to make an attempt. He moved slowly, unsure how his body would react to movement. It came back to him in pieces. Shot in the head. Bad enough. Then bit by a snake. Insult to injury.

He slid his bit leg over the edge of the bed. They had it wrapped in white linen so the color wasn't apparent, but he could see the swelling. It made his stomach roil.

Susanna came to the doorway, tying on a bonnet for her trip.

"Anything else to add to the list?"

"No, Suzy," Ruth said. "Just don't waste too much time with Harry Whitson while you're there."

Susanna looked caught. Her eyes found the floor.

"I know you're going to see him even if I tell you not to," Ruth said. "Just make it quick, okay?"

"Okay." Susanna nodded and left the room.

When Ruth turned back around The Lawyer was standing, though uneasily.

"Looks like a newborn foal," Belle said from outside the window.

"I didn't think he'd be able to run," Ruth said. "But this is a good a sign as any. Come get some food in you."

The Lawyer took several painful steps forward, wondering how far away Big Jim Kimbrough would get while he was laid up. His mind was always on his task. The hunt. He thought about it first in the morning and last at night. He thought about it before food, before sleep, before his own pain. What Kimbrough and the rest had done to him that day poisoned his blood worse than a dozen rattlers could.

"My horse …" The Lawyer started.

"She slept better than you. Ate better too. Don't you worry about her at all."

All The Lawyer worried about was when he could mount up and ride out, back on Kimbrough's trail.

* * *

Susanna spent the hour and a half ride into town watching the smoke on the ridge. Closer today than the day before. Still not close enough to worry just yet, but the way the breeze blew against her left cheek she knew the fire would continue to march toward their valley. Hopefully the river would stop the fire, but she knew sometimes all it takes is one spark.

She turned the wagon onto the main street and knew she should go see the doctor first. If she dawdled at Harry's, Ruth would be furious with her. And that man, Mr. Smith, he might die. After what he'd been through, though, she thought he must have a guardian angel with him.

Doctor Reed's house was past the church and she didn't stop until she got there. She tied off the wagon by the trough and went inside.

There was another man there. Tall and lank, with drawn features and oversized ears. He made her uneasy even from a distance. He didn't turn her way when she entered. The frightening man and Doc Reed were in some sort of negotiation.

"Look, does that cover it or not, Doc? Just tell me."

He held a leather pouch of coins in one hand. There were already three out on the table between him and the Doc.

"I suppose it does, but this is all so unusual."

"I pay my debts," the man said. There was a coldness in his voice that caused Susanna to shrink against the wall.

"Well, then consider them paid Mr. Kimbrough." Doctor Reed scooped up the coins and dropped them into a drawer in his desk, then closed the drawer sharply. He seemed eager to be rid of the tall man and turned to Susanna with a forced smile.

"Suzy, what can I do for you today?"

Mr. Kimbrough seemed to debate whether to be offended by Reed's abrupt ending of their transaction, but he merely took his time placing the hat on his head and returning his coin purse to his pocket, all while eyeing Susanna like a wolf watches a rabbit.

"I need some medicine, Doctor Reed," Susanna said. "For a bad cut and a snake bite. What can you give me for that?"

"You're snake bit?" Reed stepped closer as if to examine her.

"Oh, no, not me." Susanna put her hands out, fending off any unnecessary touching. "A guest." Embarrassed by her reaction, she turned to the stranger and found she could see Mr. Kimbrough watching them through a mirror by the door. Something about that man did not sit right with her.

Their eyes met for a split second and he turned away quickly, pretending to fuss with his hat in the reflection.

"Ruth's cousin," she said, though she didn't know what impulse made her lie. She just felt it necessary right then.

"I'll see what I can send with you, Suzy, but your guest may need my attention," Dr. Reed said.

Kimbrough left the room quickly and shut the door so hard the glass nearly broke.

* * *

Lewis was mounting his horse outside the hotel when Kimbrough approached. Creole and Spike leaned against posts on the porch like vultures too lazy to roost.

Lewis smiled nervously. "Just headed out to fetch you a lawyer's ear, Big Jim."

"Don't bother," Kimbrough said. "He ain't dead."

Lewis's face fell. "He ain't?"

Kimbrough turned to Creole and Spike. "There's a gal down at the Doc's. When she comes out, follow her. But stay back. I don't want them to know we're comin'."

CHAPTER SIX

"I told you, Harry, I have to go."

Susanna pushed the young man away from her, but not too hard. She wanted him to know she would stay if she could.

"Aw, come on. One more kiss." Harry Whitson, twenty-one-year-old son of the town's assistant bank manager, had been sweet on Susanna since she was orphaned. The strong shouldered way she stood up at the funeral of her parents and didn't cry made him see the flat-chested young girl in a new light, and he'd been smitten ever since.

"I'll be back in town soon," she said.

"You better be. I don't like the idea of you out there all alone with only women around."

She twisted her face into a soft scowl. "You saying we can't handle ourselves?"

"I'm just saying I'd feel better if there was a man around."

"A man like you I suppose?"

Susanna straightened her dress and fixed her bonnet on straight.

"Maybe, one day. But let me tell you, no woman of mine is going to have to live out in the valley on some dusty ranch. When I take over for my father at the bank, I'll have enough to build my own house right here in town."

Harry already had more money than the ranch hands and farmers because of his job as teller in the bank. Susanna wasn't attracted to his money, though. She loved his sandy hair, his pale blue eyes, his soft hands. All of the things the ranch boys weren't.

"I'm sure some woman will be very lucky indeed, then."

He held her again, his hands firm on her shoulders. "Suzy, you know it's you. When I can afford to, I'm gonna marry you and you won't have to ride for hours to get to town." He kissed her again and she nearly dropped her parcel from Dr. Reed.

"That sounds lovely, Harry. But for now, I have to get back. You know us womenfolk … can't go ten minutes without needing help with something."

She smiled as she left his embrace, and took ahold of Harry's tendered hand to steady herself as she climbed up to the wagon seat. She switched the horse into motion, and then turned to wave goodbye to Harry from over her shoulder.

On the way back to the ranch, she sang to herself. Didn't take notice of the smoke over the ridge, or even the riders following far behind.

* * *

"He said put this on his head and this one …" Susanna checked labels of the two bottles of salve Dr. Reed had given her. "And this for the snake bite."

The Lawyer sat in a chair at the long table in the middle of the main room. He kept his snake bit leg out straight—to bend it made the pain unbearable—and propped himself against the high chair back as if he might slip onto the floor at any moment.

"And with these I'll be able to leave?"

"Hold on there, cowboy," Ruth said. "You're in no shape to go anywhere. You'll stay right here for at least a week, probably two."

"Yeah," Belle said, her voice cracked with age. "What's yer rush anyhow?"

The Lawyer itched at his whiskers, grown in far longer than he liked after days without a shave. He debated how much to tell the women. He liked them, owed them his life, most likely. But they were already burdened by his presence, they didn't need to be weighed down by his past as well.

"I'm looking for someone."

"Perhaps someone who shot you? Is that it, cowboy?"

Ruth seemed to delight in needling him, but even as she did she opened the first jar of salve and prepared to apply it to his leg.

"I'm no cowboy, ma'am. I'm a lawyer, schooled and trained."

"Is that right? A lawyer."

Belle waved a dismissive hand. "Shakespeare said kill all the lawyers."

Smith was caught off guard by her knowledge of Shakespeare. He smiled. These women were full of surprises.

"I'd like to think if I represented Mr. Shakespeare he would have thought differently."

* * *

The house was hard to see in the lush green of the valley floor. From high on a ridge the four riders had been able to watch Susanna and the wagon ride down the narrow trail and to the paddock from a safe distance and now knew where to look.

"I still say we bust in there and see what's what," Lewis said. "What are they gonna say to these?" He rattled his six shooters in their holsters.

Kimbrough ignored his theatrics. "What kind of man am I, Lewis?"

Lewis ran through several ill-advised answers in his mind. *Rude. Mean. Foul smelling.* Kimbrough finally answered for him.

"Cautious."

"Yeah, cautious," Lewis agreed.

"I don't go through no door unless I know what's on the other side."

"I'm with you, Jim," Creole said. Spike nodded.

"There could be ten men down there working the land. Could be where the sheriff lives or where John Wesley Hardin takes his vacations."

Spike pushed his hat back off his forehead. "So, how do we find out, Jim?"

"You go in quiet, not loud. You go in with one rider, not four. You scout. You reconnoiter. You learn little goddamn something before you go busting in the door."

The three men nodded in agreement. Kimbrough spit.

"So Lewis, get your ass down there and learn something about that house and who's in it."

Lewis stopped nodding. "Me? Why me?"

"Because you didn't do the other goddamn job proper is why. And you'd best do this one the right way." This time Kimbrough laid a hand on his pistol, but didn't make a show of it. Just let it sit there. It was motivation enough. Lewis tugged on his reins and led his horse down the trail.

* * *

Every time Ruth touched the snake bite, The Lawyer thought he might pass out, but he kept himself from screaming which he viewed as a mountain of self-restraint.

"So what brings a lawyer out to these parts and gets himself shot?" she asked.

"Not one for polite parlor talk are you, Ruth?"

"Mr. Smith, when you've buried a husband and seen what I've seen to boot, etiquette stops making a whole lot of sense."

The Lawyer nodded. Belle and Susanna seemed eager for an answer too.

"The man I'm looking for killed my family."

The room went quiet, everyone paused in their own memory of loved ones lost.

"And you aim to bring him to justice?" Susanna asked.

The Lawyer chose not to elaborate on what kind of justice he sought. "Yes, ma'am. I do."

A firm hand knocked on the door. Everyone froze. Unexpected visitors were not the norm this far out in the valley.

"Maybe it's the doc," Susanna whispered. "He said he wanted to come check on him tomorrow."

"Doc Reed's never been early for nothing in his life," Ruth said. "Let's get Mr. Smith hid."

The Lawyer did his best to walk, but Belle slid up under one arm and helped him into the bedroom with Susanna close behind to shut the door. Ruth went to the front door, cracking it open a few inches while finding the Remington lever action rifle that sat in a crook to the left, out of sight from whoever might be at her door.

Lewis removed his hat. His haircut had gone flat, his whiskers started to reappear, but he still looked a damn sight better than the three men he left on the ridge. This woman—different from the one they followed out here—might be open to talking to him.

"Ma'am. Sorry to bust in on you like this, but my horse sure could use some water, and to tell the truth, I wouldn't say no to a bit myself." He held up his canteen, using the same ruse he'd pulled on The Lawyer.

"Trough's over to the side." Ruth gave a jerk of her chin to point the way. The door didn't open any further. "Water's clean enough for you to dip your canteen."

"I'm obliged ma'am." Lewis tried to peer around the narrow opening in the door. "Say, you mind if I talk to the man of the house. See, I'm out looking for work and if he had any need of a hand around here—"

"Is no man of the house." Ruth knew she probably shouldn't say it, but she also knew how to use that Remington. "And we don't need any help. You can get your water and be off. Town's not more than two hours ride from here."

"Off that way toward them nasty looking clouds?" Lewis pointed to the sky where it looked like piles of shearing from a black sheep. "Don't look safe to me, ma'am."

"Fires won't reach down here. River's too wide. And the town's on the good side of the river. Now if your horse and you are so thirsty, you best be filling your bellies."

"Well, now, Ma'am, I just wouldn't feel right leaving you here knowing there's no man about. Maybe I could stay a while and—"

The door swung open all the way. The Remington sat low in her arms, aimed at his gut. Her hand rested comfortably in the lever.

"I been kind. I offered you water, pointed the way. If you think we can't handle ourselves out here, mister, then your momma must have been one weak woman."

Lewis raised his hands, let his hat dangle in his left hand, his right free to make a draw if needed. Ruth kept her eyes locked on his.

* * *

"What's he doing now?" The Lawyer whispered.

Belle, staked out at the window with a Colt in her hand, whispered back. "Stepping back with his hands up. Looks like he might shit himself." She gave a breathy laugh.

Susanna stood to the other side of the window, not looking out. She held her own Colt but it looked heavy and awkward in her hand.

"What's he look like?" The Lawyer asked. "Tall? Big ears?"

"No. Skinny fella. Not much to look at."

"Said his canteen was dry?"

"Yeah."

The Lawyer cursed to himself. He turned to the bedpost and his gun belt hanging there.

* * *

"No need to get fussy, ma'am. I'll get my water and be off." He set his hat back on his head. "You ought to be careful, though. Bandits may find this trail, ma'am. Outlaws and renegades pass through these parts all the time. Some might come looking for more than a canteen full of water."

Ruth cocked the lever on the Remington. "I'll be here," she said.

Lewis tipped his hat with a smile and walked away to the trough.

* * *

"Help me," The Lawyer said. Belle and Susanna acted as crutches to move him closer to the window. From there he watched as Lewis made a show of watering his horse and filling his canteen. Lewis looked up into the paddock beside the barn where Redemption stood in all her pitch black glory, and a shit-eating grin crossed the owlhoot's face. A difficult horse to forget even if you'd seen her only once.

"Damn," The Lawyer said, low.

"You know that man?" Belle asked.

Before he could answer Susanna asked, "Is he the one you're after?"

"No. But he rides with him. And yesterday he tried to kill me."

CHAPTER SEVEN

Long after Lewis had rode off, The Lawyer sat down at the supper table though he didn't think he could eat. Worry knotted his stomach. But the savory smell of chicken and biscuits burrowed past the uneasiness he felt, and he ended up downing two plates. These women could cook as good as they nursed and farmed and ranched. The Lawyer was impressed, and full.

It hadn't sunk in until he was tucking into his second helping that he hadn't eaten much since being shot off his horse. The food brought a new focus to his thinking that had been lacking.

"It's me they're after. I need to push on from here."

Ruth cleared away his empty plate. "Mr. Smith, you wouldn't make it ten minutes down the road before you fell off your horse and into a ditch."

"You ain't moving," Belle added, her voice like an angry crow cawing.

"But they'll be back," he said.

"Not until sunup," Ruth said.

The Lawyer had learned in his short time with her, that arguing with Ruth was a fool's game. He knew better than her, however, that the most dangerous predators come out at night.

"This man, Kimbrough, you don't know what he's capable of."

"And I know damn well he doesn't know what *I'm* capable of."

Smith had to admit three women alone in a house had the element of surprise on their side when they started shooting. But tough talk and real actions were two different things. He pressed his palms against the guns on his hips. He hadn't taken them off since Lewis showed up to nose around.

"You said there was four of them, right?" Ruth asked. The Lawyer nodded. "Well, we've got four guns too. And they'll be out in the open. We've got these walls around us. That's if they decide to come. Men like that are usually cowards, prone to running."

"Ain't that why you been chasing them all over creation?" Belle said.

"Yes, but don't you see? They smell blood now. My blood. They want to end this and now they know it's only you women here. You and I might know better, but they see that as a weakness. And I couldn't live with it if the three of you got in the path of a bullet meant for me."

Ruth sat down in the chair next to him, put a hand on his knee. "That's mighty chivalrous of you, Mr. Smith. But I couldn't live with myself if I sent you out that door to your slaughter. Face it, lawyer—you're safer in here with us for the time being."

Maybe it was the belly full of food, maybe the dull pain still throbbing through his body making him weak, but he gave in. The Lawyer slumped in his chair with a sigh.

"I could go fetch Harry." Everyone turned to look at Susanna who gave a slight shrug to go along with her suggestion.

Ruth and Belle traded a look.

"He'd be another gun," Belle said. "That'd put us one up on them."

Ruth nodded. "Not a bad idea." She turned to Susanna. "Could you ride out there tonight and fetch him back by morning?"

Susanna checked the window. "Not much of a moon, not with the smoke." She pursed her lips like a little girl determined. "I could do it, though."

"You'd have to take a single horse, not the wagon."

"I'll be okay."

The Lawyer sat up straighter. "Take Redemption. She'll get you there and back in no time."

Though he didn't like the idea, he didn't have a better one. Susanna was right, that moon was having a tough time breaking through. Still red colored. Still a blood moon. It foretold trouble and it wasn't done telling.

* * *

Spike threw down his tin plate of beans.

"I bet they got good food down there." He hocked and spit, trying to get the taste out of his mouth. "I say we go right now. No use waiting 'til morning."

"Caution, Spike. Caution," Kimbrough said. He set aside his own half eaten plate of beans.

"But Lewis said it's just a woman down there."

"She lied about having that lawyer for a guest. She could be lying about other things too."

Lewis scoffed. "She wasn't lying about that Remington."

"Are you afraid of some damn woman?" Spike asked, daring him to answer anything but no.

"Hey, I'm the one who said we shoulda went in there as soon as we saw the wagon girl go inside. I ain't afraid of nothing they got in that house. She could have Mr. Remington his own self in that house and I'd still vote to go."

Creole crashed back into camp from out of the woods.

"Creole, that's the third trip tonight you took to empty your tank."

"Damn beans give me the runs. I don't understand why we can't go back to town."

Spike took the tiny stick he'd been twirling in his hand and threw it into the fire. "Or go down to that damn house and bust in. If there's a woman, there's cooking."

"Enough," Kimbrough roared. The men shut their mouths, but a few birds in nearby trees took off for a quieter roost. "You bunch of sissies been belly achin' for too damn long." He kicked his plate into the fire. "I'm hungry for some good eats too. Hell, let's go."

He stood. The others were slow to realize if he was serious. When Kimbrough put his first boot in a stirrup, they all scrambled to their feet.

* * *

Susanna took the river route, away from where they'd watched Lewis ride back up the ridge earlier. It added twenty minutes to the ride into town, but she would be more hidden on the path.

Redemption was indeed a fine mare. She took to Susanna easily with The Lawyer talking calming thoughts into her ear as Susanna mounted. They moved quickly through the trees with the sound of the river a steady companion.

Overhead the wind shifted, turning south into the valley as it did from time to time. The trees swayed, pushed by the wind rolling across the ridge and riding the slope down to the valley floor as if sucked there by the water. The wind brought with it the smell of ash from the fire and a sense of bad things to come.

CHAPTER EIGHT

The shutters rattled on their hinges, loosely covering the windows from prying eyes. The Lawyer hadn't tried for sleep yet. He sat up in the main room stoking the fire and adjusting his guns each time he moved.

Belle sat up with him, letting Ruth sleep. To his surprise she'd taken out a long pipe and packed it with tobacco. White, carved to look like ivory but probably made from bone. She smoked it slowly while rocking in a chair, blanket on her lap.

"So this man," Belle said. "He really killed your wife?"

"Would I be after a man who gave her flowers?"

"I s'pose not." She rocked. She smoked. "And you aim to bring him to trial?"

The Lawyer stared into the fire. The red orange glow of the logs looked to him like the hate in his heart. "Something like that."

Belle chuckled. "I thought so. You're a lawyer all right. Also judge and jury and executioner."

He shifted in his seat, winced in pain and tried to find a comfortable position which was nearly impossible with his aches.

"They took everything from me."

"And you mean to take everything from them," she said. "But you know …" She pulled on the pipe, let lazy smoke curl around her. She waited until he turned away from the fire and looked in her eyes. "You know what you take from them, don't mean you get yours back."

"I know."

Belle halted her rocking chair. "Well, all right, Mr. Smith. I hope to see that man meet his end right here in this valley."

He set his leg on another chair, elevating the snake bite. "I'd wager you've seen enough killing in your day with the war."

"Too much for no reason. Damn generals and such sending boys to die. I think a man who proves himself unfit to live in civilized society ought to step aside and let the rest of us live peaceably." She puffed on the pipe and let the smoke settle around her. "All that being said, so long as you know there ain't nothing out there that'll make your pain go away until you let it go."

"I'll let it go when those men are dead."

"I guess I see why you're so eager to be rid of us, then. You got a brand-new start to things at the end of your trail. I'd be anxious to get there myself. Don't be too sure you can easily let it out of your grip though. Seems to me like you got a white-knuckle hold on your hate."

He nodded. He couldn't disagree with her.

A board creaked. The Lawyer looked at Belle's rocker. Still. He held a finger to his lips with his left and slowly drew a pistol with his right. Belle set her pipe down on the table and reached for the Remington leaning there.

Another creak. Sounded like the front porch. The wind had been making strange noises through the house, though. Seams in the wood had been exposed by cold air leaking in, loose hinges revealed by the rattle of the shutters. The creaks could be more of the same, or they could be footsteps.

The Lawyer watched the wall, listening for any new sound. The breeze made a steady hum through the leaves. One of the gaps let a gust of wind in and sent the fire flickering. One of the logs fell, weakened by the burning. A bloom of sparks went up and were carried away by the chimney. The flames grew for a moment then settled down.

Behind him, he heard footsteps. The Lawyer turned in his seat, six shooter out in front of him. Ruth was there.

She held her own revolver and an alert look in her eye. She held up two fingers and pointed to the back of the house.

"Outside," she mouthed.

The Lawyer pointed to the front door and the porch beyond, hidden from their view behind the closed shutters. Another board creaked. A boot heel landed a little too hard for stealth.

The Lawyer pushed himself to standing. He grimaced with the strain, but kept any cries of pain inside. He steadied his gun at the door. The tight wrapping on his head became too much for him. He reached up and undid the bandages, unspooling the wrapper and letting it coil on the table like a snake. The air was cool on his scalp where Belle's stitches closed his wound, but his head felt better without the binding pressure of the bandage. He focused on the door again. Behind him he gestured to Ruth, pointing to Belle and urging them to both get to the back bedroom.

Belle's answer was to stand and brandish the Remington behind him. His deputy. He frowned but knew better than to argue.

The doorknob turned. A slow, testing motion. The men were being cautious, perhaps waiting for a signal from the man at the front door. The knob twisted twenty, thirty, forty-five degrees. The Lawyer raised his gun.

The door inched open. The Lawyer fired.

Wood splintered as his shot hit the door about chest height. The Lawyer was already on the move, ignoring whatever pain he felt. It was mostly masked by his pulsing adrenaline anyhow.

A loud grunt came from behind the door, then retreating steps.

"Spike, you goddamn coward," said the voice left behind. The Lawyer recognized it. He expected it to ask for a drink of water next. Lewis.

The Lawyer knew he'd hit Lewis, but stayed behind the door because he also knew Lewis had a gun. He slid himself quickly across the tiny opening in the doorway, saw Lewis crumpled there on the porch.

From the back bedroom came the sound of a window breaking, then a shot. Another. They sounded like they came from inside—Ruth fending off the attackers. From outside came a short volley of shots. The walls of the house pounded with slugs of lead burrowing into the wood.

"Call him off," The Lawyer said. He shouted so Lewis could hear him over the shots. "It's me Kimbrough wants. These women have nothing to do with it."

"I shot your ass," Lewis said. "And you was snake bit."

The Lawyer thought he sounded like he was moving farther away. He chanced a quick look out the gap in the doorway. Lewis was crawling on his belly back toward the steps.

"Those ladies kept you from dying like you was supposed to," Lewis said. "They ought to worry more about the Almighty than Big Jim. They stopped God's work from being done."

"You really think I'm gonna be carried off the heaven one day?"

"If not, save me a seat in Hell." Lewis laughed as he reached the steps. He tumbled forward and landed in the dust, clutching at the bullet wound in his chest. He'd landed on his back. Trees swayed overhead. The stars were almost blocked out by the black cloud of ash in the sky.

The Lawyer looked down at Lewis, remembering their encounter on the trail and the way he laughed when he rode away from his bullet wounded and snake bitten body.

"Why don't you save a seat for me instead."

The Lawyer fired once, straight down, to the middle of Lewis's forehead.

* * *

Belle joined Ruth in the bedroom. "The bastards," she said.

"I didn't think they'd come at night."

"I guess he does knows them better."

Ruth tried to see between the gaps in the shutters, but the night was too dark. She thought she heard horses back in the trees. They rode left and then right. How many were there? Were they circling, playing tricks?

"Mr. Smith got one of them through the door," Belle said. "He was still talking though."

The Lawyer limped into the room. "Not anymore."

"Was it your man?"

"No. The one who showed up here earlier. The one who left me to die."

"You certain he's dead?"

"I made sure of it."

"Good."

The Lawyer tried to see outside by using one of the bullets holes in the wall. Nothing but blackness.

"We can't stay here. We're sitting ducks."

Ruth held up her gun. "We already got one of them."

"Yeah, but they're out there planning. And they don't need to be quiet anymore. They'll come right at us."

"What then?" Ruth asked.

"I don't want to be here when they arrive." He looked above him. "You have an attic space?"

"Not to speak of. We'd all fit if we laid on our backs and didn't care about breathing."

The Lawyer looked around for some inspiration. "You have a barn."

"Small one next to the paddock."

"Better than nothing. They'll be focused on the house. If we can get to the barn we can get the jump on them when they attack."

Belle was shaking her head. "Long walk to that barn. Some of us don't move so fast these days."

"The dark will hide us. We need to be careful more than fast."

Ruth paced, unsure. "I'd hate to leave the house for them to do what they will."

"I'd rather it be the house than us. Besides, we'll be on them before they get in the door, long as we keep watch from the barn. Can we see well from there?"

"The front door, for sure. Not if they decide to come around back."

The Lawyer finally gave in to the pain in his leg and leaned against the door frame. "Anyone has a better idea, I'm listening."

Ruth and Belle looked to each other, then to him. Ruth shook her head, resigned. "What are we waitin' for?"

CHAPTER NINE

Spike reared back his horse and brought it a halt in front of Kimbrough.

"They got Lewis."

Big Jim kept his horse in line with one hand on the reins and his other on the stock of his Winchester. "Shit," he said. "That boy did himself in. I always knew he'd die stupid someday."

"What do we do?" Creole asked. He'd holstered his guns and leaned forward on the horn of his saddle to wait for an answer.

"Hard to tell how many guns they have in there." Kimbrough looked back down the rise to the house, half hidden in the trees. "He's inside for sure, then someone was shooting out the back."

"Damn near got me in the ass," Creole said.

"And now we're only three," Spike added.

"Well," Big Jim said as he stowed his rifle in the holster on his saddle. "I been saving this for a special occasion." He reached into his saddlebag and withdrew a single stick of dynamite.

Creole's eyes went wide. "Where'd you get that?"

"Had it for a while now. Thought maybe I'd use it to blow a safe somewheres, but I think it would be put to better use here." He smiled his crooked teeth. "Now which one of you boys has a matchstick?"

Spike and Creole stared, dumbfounded.

Kimbrough got the gist and hung his head. "Son of a bitch."

* * *

The Lawyer surveyed the yard again. No movement except for the swaying of the tress in the wind. Flakes of grey ash fell like a dusting of snow and the air smelled like dozens of campfires.

"I think it's clear."

"Maybe they moved on when one of their men was shot," Ruth speculated.

"Not likely."

"What about Susanna?" Belle asked. "She'll be back before long with that Harry in tow."

The Lawyer kept his eyes on the yard. "With any luck this will all be over by then."

"Okay, so they come back to a pile of bodies—but whose?"

The Lawyer turned to face Ruth and Belle. He made sure they were both looking at him and could see the intensity in his eyes. Reflecting the orange glow of the fireplace light, he looked lit from within. He spoke in his deepest, most stentorian voice—the one he usually reserved for closing arguments in a courtroom.

"I give you my word: no more women will die while I'm around to do something about it."

Both ladies felt the weight of what he had to say. They saw his hurt and heard his determination. They believed him.

* * *

"Wait, wait, wait, I got it." Spike pointed down to the house. "The chimney. We know there's a fire going, so we drop it down the chimney and BOOM."

A smile grew across Kimbrough's lips. "Spike, you sumbitch, you're a goddamn genius of invention."

"Let's ride."

Kimbrough's hand flew into the air to stop them from tearing off too soon. "Hold up. We need to be stealthy about this. Only one can go down there and get away with it undetected. Besides, the others need to be ready to start blasting at whoever comes spilling out that door because they're gonna be on the run faster than ants out of a hill."

Creole raised a hand. "I'll do it. When I was a kid I could climb a tree better'n a monkey."

"You got the job," Kimbrough said and tossed the stick of dynamite to him.

Creole tensed and fumbled the stick for a moment before clutching it with both hands. He exhaled deeply.

"Move out," Kimbrough commanded, and the triad eased their horses down the hill slowly.

* * *

"We should leave a note for Susanna," Belle said. "In case."

The Lawyer pursued his lips, poised to argue, but he gave in. "Fine, but hurry." He never took his eyes off the outside world, seeing movement in every shadow, danger in every swaying tree. The smell of ash in the air like a portent.

He eyeballed the distance between the front porch and the barn. A hundred paces? More? He rubbed at his leg, worrying the flesh. The skin around the twin punctures of the snake bite was still a dark purple, his foot still mostly numb. He tried wiggling his toes. They moved but it sent bolts of pain up his leg to spark out across his body. He kept his hurting from the women. His head felt fine and he saw that as a sign he was healing. Maybe when this was all over he'd still lose his leg, but that was only an argument to ride it hard like a mare you knew you'd have to shoot when the journey was through.

"How's it coming?"

"Almost there," Belle said. "Some of us didn't get as much book learning as other folks."

She stabbed a period to the end of her note and set down the pencil, then picked up her rifle. "Ready."

"Okay," he said. "I'll take the first steps out but don't wait for me. Go on past me and get there quick. I'll be moving slow."

"We can help you," Ruth said. "Get an arm under you."

"No." The Lawyer insisted and met her eyes with a strong gaze. "You keep moving. If they're waiting us out, this might be just what they want. And don't move in a straight line. You've slaughtered a chicken before."

"More than I can count," Belle said.

"Then you know what it looks like to run in a crooked line. Move like that and we'll all have a better outcome than the chicken."

The women crowded in behind him as he eased the door open a little wider.

* * *

Creole had made it on top of the roof better than if a ladder had been left there. He was almost mad the boys didn't get to see it, but they were busy moving on foot to flank the house; Kimbrough to the west and Spike to the east.

The hot air and smoke from the chimney burned Creole's nostrils when he leaned in for a look. He could hear the murmur of voices and the crackle of logs on the fire. He eyed a landing spot on the ground, planning for when he jumped. He'd land a few feet in front of the woodpile and then duck behind it for the blast. Spike and Kimbrough would be waiting it out behind a few trees, ready to spring when the blast subsided and to start shooting at the easy pickings.

"I want that lawyer," Big Jim had told them. But when the bullets stopped flying, dead is dead.

Creole set his feet to jump, then dropped the stick down the chimney.

* * *

The Lawyer pulled the door open and started limping forward in a peg-legged run. Ruth and Belle heeded his advice and went past him fast, Belle bunching up her skirts as she ran. The Lawyer swiveled his head on the lookout for trouble, a gun in each hand ready to shoot first.

Ruth planted a foot and zipped to her right, three steps later she angled left, never slowing. Belle took a more straight-line approach when it became clear Ruth was much faster. Her Remington may as well have been an umbrella. The old woman's sole focus was on making it to the barn.

The blast shattered the windows and sent glass spewing out into the yard. The Lawyer tumbled, partly from the blast of air behind him, but mostly from the startling sound of the dynamite.

Ruth let out a yelp and increased her speed. The Lawyer looked up from the ground and saw her swoop into the barn, Belle close behind.

The posts holding the porch gave way amid the damage of the blast and the front of the house sagged off into a heap. The Lawyer rolled away in the dirt.

Gunshots spat up chunks of the pathway. Flat on his back, The Lawyer extended a hand in either direction and fired a shot, his arms out like a statue of Jesus on the cross. He wanted to cover himself enough to get back on his feet and cursed his gimp leg for making it a time-consuming task. He was halfway there when another shot hit too close for him not to flinch.

He spun and fired off into the dark where the shot came from. In the paddock beside the barn the horses there were rearing back on their hind legs and neighing with fear from the blast and now the gunshots.

The Lawyer crouched low and made two stumbling steps forward. He saw movement to his left, then a flash in the dark and a bullet passed by his ear close enough for him to feel the heat. He crossed his right arm over his belly and fired. He didn't expect to hit anything at the awkward angle and while on the move, but it would buy him a few seconds which he hoped was all he'd need.

The next shot came from his right. He was flanked and still had thirty steps to go. He shot another blind cross into the darkness beyond.

"I don't give up as easy as no snake." Kimbrough's voice came out of the dark to his right. He sounded like he was enjoying himself.

Ahead, The Lawyer saw the barn door push open. Belle was there with the Remington on her shoulder, eye to the sight. She fired in the direction of the voice. Two quick shots with a pull of the lever between. She was answered by a single shot. The Lawyer saw her jerk to the side and drop the rifle. In a great poof of fabric from her skirts, Belle fell to the dirt.

Another rifle sounded, this one from far away. Down the trail came a rider firing shots to the sides of the house. Behind him The Lawyer saw Redemption and Susanna atop her. Reinforcement had arrived.

The Lawyer fired with both hands as he made the last sprint to the barn, his bad leg carving a line in the dirt as it refused to lift as high as he wanted. Susanna and her boyfriend kept firing into the darkness as they turned their horses toward the barn. Ruth opened the wide doors and let everyone inside, dragging Belle with her as she went.

CHAPTER TEN

Harry dismounted with a leap.

"Boy, you weren't fooling." He helped Susanna off Redemption, then he checked to make sure the barn doors were secure. The Lawyer had fallen to the dirt floor of the barn, pistols still in hand.

"You okay, mister?" Harry asked.

"Yeah. Check on Belle."

But Ruth was already standing over her, nervously pressing her hand against the gunshot wound. Belle had her eyes clamped shut to fend off the pain.

"Smith," Belle said. Her hand clawed at the dirt, drawing four parallel lines. "Smith."

The Lawyer turned onto his belly and crawled to her side. Belle opened her eyes into slits, saw his face close to hers.

"When you get him, tell him he didn't kill me. You tell him I died of old age. It's my time." She grabbed his lapel with a fierce grip he didn't think she could muster. "He didn't kill me, Smith. Don't you give him the satisfaction."

She let her hand unclench and laid her head down in the dirt. She smiled and showed bloody teeth. Ruth began muttering a prayer over her and then she was gone.

Susanna wept. The horses were restless and blew out breaths like little huffs of profanity. Ruth made the sign of the cross and said aloud, "Amen." Harry took off his hat and held it over his heart. He repeated, "Amen," even though he hadn't heard the prayer.

"We need to leave," The Lawyer said.

As if to prove his point, a pair of bullets hit the side of the barn. A test. Harry took the bait and went to the barn door, squeezed the barrel of his gun between a gap in the wood between the doors and fired back twice, shooting blind like a shout into the wind. Like a prayer to an empty sky.

"Hitch up that wagon," The Lawyer said. He pushed himself up to sitting and began reloading his guns. Ruth didn't argue. She stood and left Belle behind. Susanna ran to Harry and burrowed in his arms as she cried.

Harry looked at The Lawyer. "How many are there?"

"Three. I got one of them."

"Suzy says these are men of the worst kind."

He squared a gaze at the young man. "She's right." He pushed a final bullet into his gun and closed the chamber with a snap.

Ruth worked efficiently and with experience. "What was that explosion?"

"Dynamite. I don't know how much Kimbrough might have."

"Meaning we could be next in here?" Harry asked.

The Lawyer nodded. Harry hurried to Ruth's side and began helping hitch up the horse for the wagon. Susanna pulled down a horse blanket off the side of a stall and laid it over Belle. It wasn't ideal, but it was better than leaving her there in the dirt.

* * *

Creole took a slow step forward, his gun out before him like a torch leading the way. He hesitated at the corner of the house. The fire from the dynamite blast was burning on the other side, but all those gunshots had him reluctant to expose himself to the crossfire. He braved a slight lean to his right.

A gun barrel filled his vision. Creole nearly shot as he jerked back in shock, then he saw it was Kimbrough at the end of the gun.

"What are you doing sneaking around here?" Kimbrough asked.

"I was trying to get a look and see what the hell happened. I jump from the roof and hid behind the woodpile. The damn thing blew and I had to dig myself out of a cord and a half of wood."

Spike joined the party, his eyes darting and his gun anxious in his fist.

"I heard shots," Creole said.

Kimbrough nodded. "I got one of them."

"The old lady?" Spike said. "Shit, I got her."

"The hell you did."

"Right through the tit, I did."

"That was my shot and she went down and bit dirt because of it."

"You saying I can't shoot?"

"I'm saying you can't see so good."

"Either way," Creole said. "They're one down just like we are."

"No," Kimbrough shook his head. His long earlobes jiggled and beat against his neck. "There was a rider come in after."

"Two riders," Spike corrected.

"Armed and shooting."

"Well, what do we do now?" Creole wanted to know.

Kimbrough scratched at his whiskers. "Get to the horses. We'll make an injun circle around 'em. In that barn they might as well be fish in a barrel."

* * *

The Lawyer patted the mane of his trusted horse.

"I hate to say it but I can't ride." He looked at Harry. "You take Redemption. I'll ride in the wagon. We make for the trees." He turned to Susanna. "You said there's a back way to town?"

"Yes, sir. Down by the river."

"That's what we'll take, then. Only we won't turn towards town. We'll head into the hills. If they follow, they'll go toward town and miss us."

"Why not go to my house?" Harry said.

"You want to lead those men to your door?"

Harry shrank away from the question. The thought of his mother and father dead on the ground like Belle, struck him silent.

"That wagon ready to go?"

"Yep," Ruth said and she pulled herself into the seat. The Lawyer noticed she'd taken the fallen Remington from Belle.

"Susanna, you ride up front with Ruth," The Lawyer said. "I'll stay back here where I can see whoever is following. And I'll have two hands free to shoot. Harry, you stick close by. Redemption will do proud by you. Mind you she doesn't like you to shoot a gun right by her ear."

Harry stroked her mane. "Wouldn't dream of it."

"Okay, let's ride."

* * *

Kimbrough signaled with his hands, waving Spike one way and Creole the other. Three men, three guns. They took a wide approach to the barn and kept the horses at a slow trot to avoid spooking the people trapped inside. Kimbrough planned to scout the outside of the barn and see if they spotted any weaknesses, any way in. If not, then they would fire on it until they drew them out. Keep moving, keep circling. It was a technique he'd seen used by bands of Indians before when settlers holed up in a building or circled the wagons. He didn't have fifteen braves riding with him, but against a wounded man and some women he figured to do fine.

He'd made it half way around when he heard Creole shout, "They're gone."

Kimbrough and Spike caught up at the far side of the barn. The double doors swung open and the inside was quiet. Even the horses were gone, the wagon too.

Creole rode his horse over the blanket-shrouded figure on the ground. He jumped down and kicked off the blanket.

"Least we got one of them."

Kimbrough could barely make out the thin tracks of wagon wheels. He followed with his eyes as far as he could go until they faded into the darkness.

"That way."

It would be near impossible to track them at night, but if they had a wagon they'd be slower on the trail. And with the woods as thick as they were around here, Big Jim hoped for a single trail.

"How we gonna track 'em?" Spike asked.

"Best we can."

"Ain't gonna be easy."

"You'd rather sit here with a thumb up your ass?"

Spike jerked the reins of his horse and brought himself around to face Kimbrough. "I'd rather be on my way and leave this behind. No point in running toward someone intent on doing you harm."

"You goddamn coward."

"It's goddamn smart, Big Jim, and you know it."

The rising pitch of their voices began to agitate the horses.

"And what then? We wait until he comes at us next time? I'm tired of running. And he aims to do me harm, so you can fuck off to points west of wherever the hell you want to go. It's me he's been after and now that he's on the run for a change, I'm going to follow."

Creole mounted his horse and rode next to Spike.

"He's right, Spike. He won't stop coming. He's weak and his only help are a pair of women and one other rider."

Spike slapped the loose ends of his reins against his horse. "Dammit." He kicked into the horse's flank and took off after the wagon trail. Kimbrough and Creole followed.

* * *

The ride in the back of the wagon was painful. The Lawyer had been jounced around and several times landed on his injured leg. Ruth kept the wagon as straight as she could, but the trail wound around trees and the night was dark enough that the horses had trouble following the path, even when urged on by Ruth's relentless whip.

Redemption trotted alongside the wagon, sniffing the air toward The Lawyer. He figured she was wondering how he could be riding her and ahead of her in the wagon at the same time since Harry was about the same size as him.

He scoured the tree line behind them for movement. Nobody seemed to be following. He turned forward and felt encouraged by the warm glow in the night sky ahead. He felt the relief of morning dawning until he realized it was still the middle of the night and the color he saw was the fire coming down the hill.

"You see that?" he said to Harry.

"Sure do. Smell it too."

The ash in the air had been with them so long The Lawyer had gotten used to it. When he concentrated now he could tell it had gotten thicker and the air around them warmer.

"The wind must have pushed it."

The trail ahead of them dropped off as the steady undulation of the land gave way to another low hill. When Ruth crested the small rise she pulled back the horse to a stop. Ahead of them lay the ridge line ablaze in orange flames. A crooked line of fire stretched across the horizon. Below them was the river, the sounds of rising water competing now with the roar of burning timber. The fire hadn't jumped the water and didn't look to be strong enough to do so, but then no one had thought it would reach this far down into the valley.

"What do we do?" Ruth asked.

"Where does the trail go from here?"

"Cuts north along the river into town. If you want to make it to the hills, we'd have to cross at the bridge."

Susanna watched the swelling fire with wide eyes. "I'm not so sure I want to go into the hills. That doesn't look like it's stopping any time soon."

In the glow of the fire, a rolling black cloud of smoke was underlit, making a strangely beautiful moving tapestry. Columns of flame burst up and then receded. Clusters of sparks rose up and were swallowed by the cloud, like swarms of fireflies all lighting at the same time. The four of them sat and watched the world burn for a long moment.

The Lawyer asked Ruth, "If we get on that trail, we'll need to get to higher ground. Is there a way up?"

"You mean if the fire jumps the river?" The Lawyer nodded. "No," she said. "Not with the wagon. We'd be on our own to outrun the fire up the hill."

The group silently considered their options. As if to demonstrate, a family of deer came bursting out of the timber. A buck, a doe and two fawns on the run from the flames. The deer crashed through the woods, snapping tree limbs and swiftly changing direction in a run for their lives. Two deer split left around them and the others split right. In a great cacophony of hooves and snapped twigs they came and then were gone, leaving the forest to be filled with only the distant sound of rushing water and the low rumble of fire on the ridge across from them.

Then a bullet split the night air.

At first The Lawyer had the absurd thought that hunters were after the deer. But a second shot sent a spray of bark from a tree very near Harry's head and they all knew at once they'd been found by Kimbrough.

CHAPTER ELEVEN

"Move. Now!"

Ruth whipped the horse and the wagon jumped. The Lawyer fell to his side, a splinter piercing his forearm from the planks of the wagon bed.

Harry urged Redemption to follow and quickly they were tilted forward on the way down the ridge to the river below.

The hooves of the approaching horses were more steady and heavier than the deer had been. Kimbrough and his men were focused on the hunt, into the inferno from where the whitetails were running in fear.

Kimbrough didn't waste any bullets trying to fire at a moving target from horseback. He must have known they had speed to their advantage.

The Lawyer sat up in the back and tried to catch sight of his hunters. A revolver in each hand, he waited for a shot to present itself. He knew his skills as a marksman were good, but he wouldn't shoot unless he knew he could knock a man from his mount. He figured it must have been one of Kimbrough's hired guns who'd taken a pot shot at them. Kimbrough himself would have been smarter than to shoot from as far away as they still were.

The sound of the river grew louder until the trail turned to the right and they found themselves riding alongside the wide stretch of water. The ground was still steadily falling away at this part of the valley so the water moved swiftly and the banks churned white as rocks and tree roots blocked the way.

Another shot zinged past them. The Lawyer could make out three shapes in the distance, like phantom horsemen in a children's tale. The world around them was growing brighter as they moved north. The fire had descended the ridge almost to the water here.

Harry kept Redemption close by the side of the wagon, never wanting to be far from Susanna's side. That left a clear and open shot for The Lawyer, if he could get any sense of aim from the bouncy bed of the wagon.

He fired at the shapes coming closer. All three kept on charging.

"Susanna, you have that rifle?" he called out.

She turned in her seat with the Remington in her arms. Without being asked she raised the gun to her shoulder and took aim at the shapes. The riders appeared to emerge from the darkness as if being born of the flames. The firelight cast them in a hellish red.

Susanna fired. The riders didn't slow.

"The bridge," Ruth shouted.

The Lawyer turned. Ahead was a covered bridge it's sides engulfed in flames from a tree that had fallen near it, making a tunnel of flame.

"Take it," The Lawyer said.

"What?" Ruth asked.

"Take the bridge. If we can make it and leave them behind, it may be our only hope."

Two quick shots rang out. One bullet sent splinters flying from the sideboard of the wagon. Ruth snapped her whip and yelled, "He-ya!"

The Lawyer fired twice behind him and Harry turned in the saddle and shot toward the approaching men. The Lawyer saw them veer off and cut some speed from their approach. He hoped it would be all they needed.

Ruth knew better than to have the horse slow down at all before making it across the bridge. If she gave the animal a moment's hesitation it would never cross onto the burning planks. She kept up a steady crack with the whip as she began a wide turn.

The Lawyer called out to Redemption. "Follow, girl. Follow."

A fresh volley of gunshots cut through the noisy roar of the fire. Kimbrough must have known what they were attempting and wanted to stop them. Even if Ruth pulled back the reins now there was no going back. The wagon dove into the tunnel of fire.

The heat was staggering. It fell on them like a burning blanket. Susanna covered her face and curled into a ball on the seat. Ruth hunched over but never stopped whipping or calling out to the horse. The Lawyer lay flat and felt the heat wrap around him and press hot against his face.

Harry urged Redemption on. The mare called out her pain and fear in whinnying cries but never slowed.

The pounding of hooves, the rattle of the wagon wheels, the trapped angry screaming of the fire made for the loudest sound The Lawyer had ever heard and then, like a bucket of cold water, they were out into the night air again.

Around them the woods were on fire, but up in the trees, not on the ground. Ruth tugged at the reins and steered the wagon to the right to follow the path toward town. The wagon wood creaked and smoke puffed from some planks that had gotten a little too close to the flames inside the tunnel. The wagon lifted onto two wheels and The Lawyer had to hold on to keep from falling out.

"Suzy, hang on!" Harry shouted. Susanna screamed and gripped the bench as the wagon tipped and then righted itself. Back on the path, there was barley room to move the wagon, room to turn and look back.

The bridge started a slow collapse into the river. First the roof of the covered bridge fell in. That brought the bottom out and finally the sides gave way. The wood planks dove into the water as if they were trying to save themselves from the pain of the burning. One by one the planks went out and the charred remains were carried away down the river.

On the banks of the far side, Kimbrough and his two riders stood.

There was no time to celebrate as all three men began firing on the lucky four who'd made it across.

Ruth whipped the wagon forward again as Harry shot back and The Lawyer got to his knees, firing until his guns were empty.

The trail curved up and away from the river the wagon cut a swath through a burning landscape, fleeing one hell for another.

CHAPTER TWELVE

Kimbrough cursed God and the Devil both, but his cries were swallowed by the noise of the river and the cracking of timbers as the bridge fell into the river. Each burning plank that fell gave off a mocking hiss as it hit the rushing water.

The fire seemed to stand on the edge of the river. It raged, echoing Kimbrough's curses into the night. Trees burned tall columns of flame that disappeared into the night sky, but the fire did not jump the river. It howled a final note as the fire met its match in the water.

"What now?" Spike asked.

Kimbrough struggled to rein in his horse who bucked and whined at the wall of heat coming at them. "We need to stop them before they get to town."

"How do we do that without a goddamn bridge to cross?"

"We head back on the other trail and ride like hell."

"What if we don't cut them off?"

"Then we'll get them in town. I don't care if I have to kick in every door or burn down every building—they ain't getting away."

Kimbrough holstered his gun and spurred his horse back in the direction they came from. Spike and Creole traded a head-shaking look and seemed to have a conversation with their eyes, wondering when was too much with Kimbrough. Not enough yet, they decided without a word and fell in behind him on the long trek retracing their steps.

* * *

Ruth drove the horse hard. Panicked and lost the stallion pulled the wagon up into the charred aftermath of the fire. The ground grew tendrils of smoke like tall grasses and the trees around them were shrouded in black charcoal. Occasionally they passed a tree that somehow managed to avoid the blaze. The trail vanished into the black carpet of ash below them.

A fallen tree bucked the wagon and The Lawyer nearly bounced out. Susanna yelped and Harry called out to her, "Hang on, Suzy, hang on."

They rose up and out of the flames entirely and the world became shades of black all around them. The Lawyer was about to call for Ruth to slow the wagon when they hit a deep rut and the right front wheel cracked. The wagon tilted sharply as the wheel threw spokes and their forward momentum stopped abruptly. The Lawyer was launched over the broken wheel, Ruth and Susanna pitched forward and bounced off the horse to land on the forest floor of black ash and hot cinders.

Harry called Susanna's name and leapt from Redemption.

The Lawyer rolled over and sent a small cloud of ash up around him. His head throbbed again and his leg seared with pain, but nothing new was broken.

Harry reached Susanna where she lay beside the broken wheel with Ruth draped over her legs. They both had cushioned their fall on the backside of the horse and were unharmed. The horse continued to pull and buck at his leads. Harry, once he knew Susanna was all right, went to calm the horse.

"Mr. Smith!" Ruth called.

"I'm okay."

She followed his voice and found him in the ashes. The ground below him was warm.

"Some mighty fine driving there, ma'am."

Ruth turned her eyes away. If her face wasn't so smeared with black ash, he'd swear she was blushing.

"Right up until that last part."

"Can they follow us?" he asked.

"Next crossing is more than two miles upriver. Unless they wanted to swim the river, they're shit outta luck." She looked away again. "Excuse me."

"Then we can lay low and take stock." He called out, "Harry, how's Susanna?"

"I'm fine," she answered for herself.

He heard a familiar snuff. Redemption was walking close to him, following his voice. She was breathing hard, white foam in the corners of her mouth. She bent to sniff him and The Lawyer patted her long nose. It was like greeting a long lost friend.

* * *

A half hour later they had the wagon horse unhitched and hobbled on a nearby tree, the wagon more or less straightened out, though the wheel was beyond repair, and an inventory of all their remaining weapons and ammunition.

"It's late," The Lawyer said. "It's been a hell of a day and we're all tired. I say we bed down here and come morning I'll ride into town and see about getting a new wagon to come get us out of here."

"Sleep sure does sound good," Susanna said, "but are you sure they won't come back?"

"I'll keep watch," Harry said. Suzy smiled and leaned her head on his shoulder, her brave man.

"We'll take shifts, Harry and I," The Lawyer said. "Morning can't be too far away and I'll want to get an early start. These horses need water maybe more than we do and with daylight Kimbrough will be on the move again, most likely."

"You don't think he moved on?" Ruth asked.

"He may have. But seeing his eyes last night, I feel like he's ready for this to come to an end."

"Oh, I hope he does run away like the coward he is," Susanna said.

Ruth put a hand over her heart and said quietly, "Belle."

It was all the eulogy she needed. Everyone lowered their heads and fell silent. Susanna leaned harder into Harry and cried. He looked at The Lawyer over her head and said low, "I'll take first shift. You get some rest."

The Lawyer nodded his thanks and stretched out in the back of the wagon next to Ruth. Susanna slept sitting up in Harry's embrace on the wagon's seat. The heat rising from the forest floor after the flames had passed made it a bearable night out in the open.

* * *

Harry let The Lawyer sleep through the night. When he woke he found himself in a scorched wasteland. Now that the black cloud of smoke had moved on, the daylight could finally cut through to the forest floor and it lit up a black coating of ash over everything, tall trees like burnt matchsticks surrounding them and an eerie lack of bird calls or movement.

"My God," he said under his breath.

"I know," Harry said. "Pretty frightening."

Ruth and Susanna were still asleep. In the morning light The Lawyer could see the soot smeared on their faces from the rough night and harrowing escape. He'd never again doubt the strength of a woman.

"I'll ride into town," he said as he stood on stiff legs. "I'll arrange for a new wagon to be brought up here with a fresh team of horses. Then I'll make sure the undertaker rides out to the house to tend to Belle."

"I appreciate it, Mr. Smith. Would it be better if I went?" Harry said, looking at The Lawyer's leg.

"No. Better you should stay here with them." The Lawyer reached up and scratched his scalp. Dried blood stuck under his nails from his wound. He hadn't even noticed it bleeding last night. Thinking of mounting Redemption and riding for the first time in days made him aware of his missing hat. Left behind at Ruth's place, he felt naked without it but lucky to be alive.

Redemption huffed as if in greeting when his familiar weight mounted the saddle. He checked the load in both pistols.

Harry stood to see him off. "Are you sure, Mr. Smith, you're not going into town to find that man on your own?"

Did it show on him? Was it that obvious? Or had it simply been so long that he'd ridden with murder in his heart that now it showed on his face like a permanent scar?

"I want to see to it that you all are safe before I start tracking Kimbrough again."

"But you will continue after him?"

"It's my job."

"I thought your job was lawyering."

"Call it my vocation then. Bullets, snakes, the very fires of hell won't keep me from bringing that man and all his kind to justice."

Harry patted Redemption on the flank, a gentle thank you for her bravery the night before. "Mr. Smith, I do believe you—you've proven it with all three of those trials brought down on you in the last few days. I believe you have God on your side, sir, and that you shall be victorious."

The Lawyer turned Redemption to face the trail down the hill. "Son," he said, "God turned his back on me a long time ago when he allowed the murder of my family. He surely won't approve of my intentions and he no doubt frowns on the ones in my wake. But I don't concern myself with what God wants or whose side he's on. I'd rather know my guns are loaded than my soul is saved."

He heeled into Redemption and they rode away, down the hill, kicking up a trail of ash to mark their way.

CHAPTER THIRTEEN

Kimbrough had spent a fitful night sitting up outside the post office waiting for that damned lawyer and women to ride into town. Spike and Creole fell asleep against the side of the building and took turns snoring, one louder than the other. At one point a pair of rats came along and Kimbrough watched them crawl all around the slumbering men picking crumbs from their scruffy beards.

He was cold in his bones and angry everywhere else. He kicked at Spike's boot.

"Get up, dammit."

Spike jerked awake and brought Creole awake with him. They each looked no better than a dried out animal skin and they moved slow and sleepy to start the day.

"Did they show?" Creole wondered aloud.

"Yeah," Kimbrough said, his voice dripping with poison. "I took care of 'em all by myself. Didn't want to wake you two sleeping beauties."

"Sorry, Big Jim. We was tired."

"I figured that from all the snoring."

"So what's next?"

"I need to warm up, then I'm going after them."

He stood and stretched his achy bones. Spike and Creole stayed on their asses. Spike wiped crust from his eyes. "Up into the hills?"

"If they didn't come down here then they're still up there."

"Maybe the fire got 'em."

Kimbrough spun on his boot heel and bent down to snarl at them through gritted teeth. "Then I want to see their charred goddamn corpses."

He stood and turned again, then walked down the boardwalk without waiting.

Spike turned to Creole. "He's gone loco."

"He was that first day we met him."

"I don't know about this anymore."

"Me neither."

Despite their talk, both men stood and followed. They caught up to Kimbrough outside the saloon where Big Jim pounded on the door with the side of his fist. The banging carried down the street and Spike kept looking to see who might come out first and tell them to stop.

"I don't think they're open, Big Jim."

"I don't give a good goddamn. I want a drink."

He kept up his relentless hammering until the bartender came to the door in a red union suit and hair askew.

"Door's closed, dammit. That means we ain't open." His puffy eyes registered the long face and droopy earlobes of the man who'd pinned his cravat to the bar a few nights back. He came awake quickly after that and tried to shut the door again. Kimbrough gave it a kick and pushed his way inside. Spike and Creole followed if only to get off the street and avoid any more unwanted attention.

"Gimmie a drink," Kimbrough said, clapping his hands and rubbing them together to get the blood flowing.

"It–it–it's early yet …"

Kimbrough stopped on his march to the bar, turned and gave the barman a look out from under his brow that could've spoiled milk and turn back a charging bull. Slowly, as if he wanted the barman to make note of each movement of his arm, Kimbrough drew his long Bowie knife and held it out straight.

"Last time I was here I thought we came to an agreement."

"I–I guess I could pour you one."

The barman hurried around the counter, his bare feet shuffling on the sawdust covered floor. He grabbed the first bottle he saw and filled a glass with brown liquor. Kimbrough stepped up and spiked the knife into the bar, lifted the glass and drained it, keeping his eye on the barman the whole time. He pushed the glass back for a refill. The barman didn't argue.

Spike and Creole had another wordless conversation. Spike nodded slightly and cleared his throat.

"Big Jim, we was thinkin' …"

Kimbrough didn't turn. He threw back his second drink, pushed the glass forward again.

"… we think it's time we moved on."

Kimbrough kept his eyes toward the bar. "Is that right?"

Creole stepped in with a nervous waver in his voice. "We're holding you back is all. I think you'd do better riding alone for a spell, don't you think?"

"Can't handle it, can you?"

"No, it's not that. Ain't we done you right so far?"

"And now you're doing me one final favor? Is that it?"

The barman poured the last of his bottle into the glass then took two steps back.

"It's better this way, don't you figure?"

Kimbrough turned. He lifted the glass and gave a crooked half smile. "That's mighty white of you boys." He sipped at the drink more slowly this time, but still emptied the glass before it left his lips. He turned back to the barman who nervously watched.

"A little light on that last pour, wasn't you?"

The barman held up the empty bottle. "Last of the bottle, sir."

Kimbrough set the glass down with a crack. Paused. Picked the knife out of the bar and reached. Trapped by the narrow space behind the bar, Kimbrough grabbed the barman by his union suit in one hand and pulled him halfway across the bar. He put the knife to the barman's throat.

"You got more back there, ain't ya?"

The barman started to speak but his throat moving on the edge of the knife caused him pain and a thin trickle of blood. He nodded almost imperceptibly.

"Well," Creole said. "I guess we'll be going now."

"Wait," Kimbrough said. "Don't you even want a farewell drink with me?"

He still held the barman at knife's end and the two henchmen looked at each other as if debating whether to run or have that drink. They walked to the bar and could see the terror in the barman's watery eyes.

Kimbrough released him.

"A drink for my friends."

After putting a hand to his throat to check for damage, the barman brought two more glasses up and broke the seal on a new bottle. He spilled whiskey on the bar as he poured three sloppy shots.

Kimbrough raised his glass and nodded without saying a word. Spike and Creole mimicked him and all three threw down their shots. When he set the glass back on the bar, Kimbrough lifted the nearly full bottle by the neck and held it in his fist. He swung it and smashed the barman across the cheek with it, shattering the glass and spraying cheap whiskey down the counter.

Spike and Creole stepped back. The barman went down, screaming. Kimbrough calmly took three coins from his pouch and set them on the bar. He leaned over and said to the injured barman, "Don't let nobody say I don't pay for what I drink."

With a tip of his hat, Kimbrough turned and walked past Spike and Creole out the door.

CHAPTER FOURTEEN

It felt good to be back in the saddle atop Redemption. The Lawyer had picked his way slowly down the ridge into town, a ride that took more than two hours. As he turned onto the main street his eyes darted side to side in search of the familiar drawn features of Big Jim Kimbrough. A woman stepped from the general store laden with packages. A man exited the barber shop running a hand over his newly smooth chin. In the alley beside a restaurant a man tossed a bucket of dirty water onto the ground.

No Kimbrough.

The Lawyer stopped at the livery and made arrangements for a fresh wagon and three horses to head back up the trail to get Ruth, Susanna and Harry.

"I won't be able to send someone for another hour or two, though," said the liveryman. "My errand boy is out at the Merrill place right now."

"Make sure he brings some extra canteens when he goes. Full ones."

"Will do, mister. You was mighty lucky to make it up there on that ridge last night, what with the fire burning through."

"We did better than if we'd stayed in the house."

"That right? Done in, huh?"

The Lawyer thought about the dynamite blast. "That's right. Done in." He made a motion to put his hat on his head, realizing again he'd lost his stovepipe back at Ruth's. "Would you tell me which way to the undertaker."

The liveryman looked stricken. "Did some of your kin die in the fire?"

"Someone close to me passed last night, yes." Like a lawyer, he spoke something less than the truth but more than a lie.

"Damn sorry to hear it." The liveryman gave him directions and swore to have his boy out with the new wagon as soon as he was back.

* * *

As he approached the undertaker's shop, he saw the familiar smear of greased down hair on top of the man dressed in black as he moved a freshly made coffin to lean against the side of the building beside a sign that read: DEATH SERVICES $1.75 BOXES $2.00 in hand painted letters. He remembered back several days to when he met him on the trail and wondered if the man would recognize him.

"Morning," The Lawyer called.

The undertaker looked up, his shoulders hunched. He hadn't noticed it on the trail and with the undertaker in the seat of his wagon, but the man was slightly hunchbacked.

"And to you."

"I need to make arrangements."

The undertaker took out a small pad of paper and a pencil from his coat pocket. "Who's the deceased?"

"Her name was Belle. She's out at a ranch house in the valley."

He looked up with one eye squinted. "I gotta pick her up?"

"Well, that's where she is, so …"

"Cost you an extra dollar."

"I want it seen to that she gets a good and proper burial here, in town. There are people coming who know her full name. And I want services read over her. I don't want you to take her to where the unnamed go to rest."

A spark of recognition came into his one open eye. "I remember you. Don't suppose it'd do me any good to offer you that dollar back in exchange for helping me dig?"

He gestured with his thumb at his hunchback, trying to elicit some sympathy for the pain of digging.

"You picked a rotten line of work, mister."

"Death is rotten. Ain't no way 'round it. Nothing but rotten the whole way through." He smiled his damaged teeth. "Pay's good though. And I never run out of customers."

"You seem pleased with the idea."

"Fact of life. If I had any skills toward it, I'd help women birth their babies too. Get 'em on both ends. Plus, you get to see them women without their drawers on. 'Course, you get to see under their britches in my line too, but it's not quite the same thing, is it?"

The Lawyer gave the undertaker a sour look to match his opinion of the man. He reached into his pocket and took out a coin pouch. After paying the man, he looked up he caught sight of another familiar face. It wasn't Kimbrough but the two sidekicks riding with him. He quickly pocketed the pouch and turned Redemption to the south where the two men were walking away from a shop advertising GRIDDLE CAKES, EGGS, HAM STEAKS, COFFEE.

"How many of those boxes have you got?"

The undertaker followed The Lawyer's gaze, saw the two men's backs. "Enough," he said.

"Put them on my tab." He heeled into Redemption and trotted away. The undertaker scratched at his humpback and laughed to himself. Business was going to be good this week.

* * *

"Hold up there, boys."

Spike and Creole both turned with one hand on the grip of their guns, but when they saw The Lawyer with his revolver trained on them, both men froze before they drew.

"Where's Kimbrough?"

"We don't know," Spike said. "Out lookin' for you I 'spect."

"Out lookin' where?"

"Back up the mountain. Least that's what he said. We split ways."

"Since when?"

"Since this morning."

Creole said, "That man is crazy. But I don't gotta tell you that, mister."

The Lawyer kept his gaze steady and his voice steadier. "You were riding with him."

Sweat beaded on both men's foreheads. Spike held his hands out in front of him as if he were calming a spooked horse. "That was before we knowed what type of man he is."

"We got no beef with you, mister," Creole said.

"You came with Kimbrough to kill me at the ranch house. And you killed Belle who showed me great kindness. That makes you a friend to my enemy and an enemy to my friends." He drew back the hammer on his gun. "That makes you guilty."

"Now, now, now, mister—"

From behind The Lawyer came an angry voice. "Hey, you sons a' bitches!"

Keeping his gun on them, he turned Redemption sideways so he could see who approached. His other hand went to his second gun. The owner of the shack selling griddle cakes was out in the street still wearing his grease-stained apron.

"You get back here and pay for them hotcakes you ate."

It was enough spark to start the fire. Spike drew first and shot at the cafe owner. Creole took aim at The Lawyer. He was already backing up Redemption and he fired a shot that hit Spike in the stomach.

Behind them in the street the cafe owner scrambled, unhurt, on his hands and knees through the dirt to get back to his shop. From a safe vantage point with his one eye on the action, the undertaker watched for fun from the doorway of his soon-to-be-busy shop.

Spike fired off three rounds from down in the dirt where he'd fallen. He wasn't looking where his slugs landed. He was angry, in pain, and wanting to shoot anything.

Creole was on the run, hugging close to the buildings as he ran. The Lawyer took another shot at Spike and with more time to aim he silenced the man's shooting and cries of anguish with a well-placed bullet to the head. When he looked up, Creole had disappeared around the corner.

He jolted Redemption to action and followed, nearly trampling Spike's sprawled legs as they ran. He turned the corner but saw no one. The street was empty. A door slammed shut in the distance. Behind him a woman screamed at seeing Spike lay dead. The Lawyer urged his horse forward, scanning the street for Creole on an ambush.

If Kimbrough was headed back up the ridge, seconds mattered. He had a head start and if he reached Ruth and the others before The Lawyer could get there, they were helpless against Kimbrough's merciless ideas of revenge. He wasn't sure how much time he should waste looking for Creole.

A quick rumble of hooves sounded and a horse streaked past The Lawyer farther up the street. Creole was on the run at a serious gallop. He rode high in the saddle, whipping the horse at the neck and riding away from the direction of the ridge. The Lawyer decided to let him go.

An eerie flashback played in his mind. It forced its way in, no matter how hard and for how long The Lawyer had spent trying to keep it out. Drenched in darkness and spiked with pain, he thought of his family—dead. He hadn't been home when his wife and children were slaughtered. He only saw the aftermath of what Kimbrough and the others did. He didn't intend to let that happen twice.

CHAPTER FIFTEEN

Ruth stroked the mane of her horse, wishing she had a proper brush. All around them the landscape was charred black, and the absence of animal chatter made the scene like something out of a dream. The smell in the air however returned reality.

Ruth climbed to the top of the ridge, a few hundred feet from where the wagon had crashed. From there she could see for miles, the scar of the fire across the land reached the horizon. For Ruth, it felt like looking into the past. Her life before—gone. The new life she'd rebuilt, now blown up and burned down. Her friend, Belle, killed for another man's vengeance.

She would do it again, she decided. Taking in Mr. Smith and nursing him back to health was the right thing to do. To help those in need. She hadn't been to church since she buried her husband, but she kept her thoughts on right and wrong. On charity and empathy. Smith needed her help and that's what she was on this earth to do. Lord knows it wasn't for ranching. She'd turned out to be lousy at that. If the women hadn't been good at raising enough crops to eat and mending their own clothes, there's no way they could have survived these years on the paltry sums they took in from their skinny herd.

"Miss Ruth?"

Susanna stood a few feet down the ridge looking up at her.

"Yes, Suzy?"

"Harry and I are going to walk for a bit. He says he wants to talk."

Ruth smiled. "I'll bet he does."

"We won't be far, I promise. When Mr. Smith gets back you can just holler and we'll come straight away."

"You two take your time. I think Mr. Smith won't be returning all too soon. May seem he's been gone for hours, but I suspect it hasn't been that long." She looked at the sun's position in the sky. Not even noon yet.

"Thanks."

"Do holler if that boys tries to get fresh. I still have that Remington, you know."

"Harry? Why, he'd never!"

"I've yet to meet a man who could say never. Now run along."

Susanna turned and walked down to the broken wagon where Harry waited. Ruth looked back out over the charcoaled landscape and thought about her own ruined past.

* * *

They laughed as Harry held her hand and kept up a quick pace through the woods. With all the branches burned off the trees they made good time down the ridge toward the river.

"Slow down, Harry."

"I wish I had a picnic."

"I wish I had a drink of water."

"When we reach the river you can drink all you want."

"If I don't faint before we get there."

He laughed and pulled her along faster.

A few moments later they could hear the water. They slowed and walked the rest of the way, their fingers entwined. When they reached the bank Harry unbuckled his gun belt and set his revolver on the ground. He leaned over and dipped the holster in the water and brought it back, full and leaking like crazy.

"Hurry now."

Susanna drank, leaning forward at the waist and trying in vain not to let the dripping water splash her dress. Harry refilled the holster and handed it to her twice more before taking a drink himself.

"It tastes like leather," she said.

"But you're not thirsty any more are you?"

"No," she said with a smile.

"Suzy," Harry dropped the holster to the ground. He took both her hands in his. "I want to talk to you. To ask you something, actually."

"What, Harry?"

"The idea of you living out there in the valley, of what happened yesterday and how far away I was. I wasn't there to help you."

"That's not your fault, Harry."

"I know it wasn't, but still. I don't like the idea of you being so far away. Without me. So I wanted to know … to ask you …"

He dropped to one knee. Susanna covered her gaping mouth and felt tears brim in her eyes.

"Will you marry me, Susanna? Let me take you away from this. Let me protect you in our own house, in town. Let me take care of you."

"Oh, Harry, yes, yes, yes!"

He stood and they embraced. It wasn't Harry who got fresh. Susanna pulled him close and leaned into him with a kiss.

* * *

Ruth stepped through the ashes to the wagon, still tilted and lame.

"No place for a woman alone."

The voice startled her. She looked up to see a man on horseback, how he'd gotten there without her seeing him she didn't know. Her thoughts had been far away and as she walked she'd been looking down at the powdery ground.

"I'm not alone," she said, eyes searching the burned out trees for Harry and Susanna, or Mr. Smith.

She didn't know him on sight, but her gut told her this was the Jim Kimbrough that Smith had mentioned. With a smug grin on his face and his coat pushed aside exposing his gun for easy drawing, Ruth felt unsettled.

He made a show of turning his head from left to right. "You look alone to me."

"The others are around. And more coming. A new wagon with horses." Her eyes landed on the Remington propped up against the wagon seat where she'd left it. "The sheriff, too."

The lie didn't seem to register with Kimbrough. He kept right on leering.

"I can help you. Take you down the mountain into town and get you fixed up with a new wagon in no time."

"That won't be necessary. Like I said, I got people waiting on me and they're bound to be back here any moment."

In a flash the gun was in his hand. "I wasn't asking, miss."

CHAPTER SIXTEEN

The Lawyer stopped to let Redemption drink from a stream. He'd been riding her to the limit and he needed a break as much as she did. His leg ached and the bandage was coming undone. The flesh below had gone from a dark purple to an unripe plum color with splotches of sour peach. The two fang marks were still black and raised, but he took any sign of pain in his leg as a good one. Pain meant the leg was still alive and wouldn't have to be removed.

He left the saddle and filled his canteen from the stream, working side by side with Redemption as they had for so long. He took a drink, topped off the canteen, and remounted while she still drank.

His head felt fine—if not a little naked without his hat—but the wound along his skull was healing nicely thanks to Belle's stitch work. He wiped sweat from his brow as he looked up the trail rising into the charred hills. No signs of Kimbrough or any other living thing.

Redemption lifted her head, thirst satiated, and he spurred her onward up the ridge.

* * *

Susanna was eager to share the news with Ruth who'd been the closest to a mother since her own had died—though she knew Ruth would rather be considered a big sister. Either way she wanted her to be the first to hear of the engagement.

The walk up the hill had taken longer and more breath than their run down, but Harry and Susanna never let go of each other's hand.

They reached the broken wagon and saw the horse still hobbled to a tree, but no Ruth.

"Ruth?" Susanna kept walking to the top of the ridge where she'd seen Ruth looking out over the far valley. Not there, either.

"Harry, do you see her?"

"No."

Susanna stood and puzzled for a moment. Harry called to her. "Suzy, look."

She saw him staring at the ground. "What is it?" She started back down to him.

"Looks like someone was here. All this disturbed ash. No way our horse could have done it, and Mr. Smith left from the north edge of the trail. Someone on horseback came by here."

"Maybe Mr. Smith came back."

"Maybe."

But Susanna knew what was going through his mind. "Then why didn't they call out for us?"

"Exactly."

"You don't think …?"

"I don't know what to think, but I don't like it."

"Oh, Harry, if something happened to Ruth …"

He followed the hoof prints for a few feet. "They went this way. Come on."

He untied the horse and climbed up. He reached out a hand for Susanna and swung her up behind him where she wrapped her arms around his waist.

"Wait," she said. Bending to the side while holding his belt to keep herself on the horse, she stretched a long arm toward the wagon seat, grabbing hold of the Remington, then she sat up straight. Harry nodded his approval and snapped the reins, driving the horse along the footsteps in the ash.

* * *

The Lawyer couldn't shake the memories. He feared coming upon Ruth and Susanna slaughtered just as his wife and daughter were. He knew he would see their bodies, but his own family's faces. Redemption picked her way higher up the ridge. The sun shone bright with no leaves to shade the trail. And without his hat the glare blinded him. Between that and the shroud of memories, he didn't see the horse approaching.

The gunshot snapped him to attention. It passed by his hip, piercing his newly filled canteen which spouted a stream of water from the hole.

The Lawyer drew his gun and found himself facing Kimbrough at last. He and his mount were thirty feet up the trail, too far for Kimbrough's shot to be accurate, but well within The Lawyer's range—if Ruth hadn't been serving as a shield for Kimbrough.

He had an arm wrapped around her, the reins in his fist as he pulled her tight to him. His shooting hand was outstretched past her body, another reason his shot had missed the mark. He wasn't looking down the barrel with her in the way. He'd missed his chance to end it quickly.

"Let her go, Kimbrough."

"Y'know, you've been doggin' me for so damn long I just about believe you *would* shoot her to get to me. Just about."

"She's got nothing to do with this."

"Then you shouldn't'a moved into her place."

"She was just trying to keep me alive."

"Puttin' off the inevitable, I'd say."

Ruth drew short, shallow breaths. Sweat rose on her face, her knuckles white where she gripped his arm. Her eyes fixed on The Lawyer.

"Where are Susanna and Harry?" he asked.

Ruth answered, "They're fine. He only took me."

Kimbrough jerked her closer. "Did I say you could talk?"

"Kimbrough, I aim to make you pay for what you did," The Lawyer said.

"What I did?" Kimbrough mocked. "With all I've done, you got to be more particular than that."

The Lawyer felt his face flush. For the incident that changed his life to be of such little importance to Kimbrough, it struck deeper than the bullet across his scalp.

"You killed my wife, my children. For no good goddamn reason. You took everything from me."

"The half breed? She was your wife? Shit, there must have been five or six of us—"

"Get down and fight like a man!" The Lawyer dismounted. He stood, ready.

"You want to draw against me, is that it? I don't think we need to bother. Seems like I got you over a barrel, mister. And I'm sick and goddamn tired of you chasin' me all over creation. Time for me to do what that fool snake couldn't."

The Lawyer saw Kimbrough's arm extend, his hand contract. It was enough of a tell for him to start moving. When the shot came, The Lawyer was gone, rolling away, covering himself in ash.

Ruth pushed at Kimbrough's arm. She grunted with the effort and twisted her body at the same time, slithering away from his grip. She fell from the saddle and landed hard on her back, the wind knocked out of her. But Kimbrough's focus was on The Lawyer. He fired twice more, chasing him over the charcoal-covered ground as The Lawyer rolled and rolled, layering himself in more soot.

Spooked by the commotion, Kimbrough's horse reared back and tugged at the bit. The Lawyer came to a stop and fired, just missing the balking horse.

Another shot burst from the woods down the trail. The Lawyer stayed flat on his belly and looked up to identify the new arrival thundering on horseback toward them. Creole. Must have followed him. The desperado took potshots that punched the ground, as if he wasn't aiming at anyone.

The Lawyer saw a fallen tree a few feet away. He crawled for it, ash choking him as he stirred up the powdery residue.

Kimbrough took another shot, closer this time.

Ruth got her air back and crawled away from the horse's legs stomping around her. She made it to a blackened tree stump and curled behind it.

The Lawyer made it to the tree. He slid over the trunk and tucked behind it as one of Kimbrough's slugs kicked up a puff of black char.

Creole called out. "Kimbrough, I want him. He killed Spike."

"He's mine, goddammit."

A shot rang out but The Lawyer couldn't tell whose it was. He dared a peek over the top of the log and saw Creole riding closer, his eyes wild with hate.

Another blast, this time from a rifle. The Lawyer turned and saw yet another rider joining the fight. Harry came storming in with Susanna right behind him, the Remington in Harry's hand.

Creole sat straight in his saddle and squeezed off a round. Harry's body jerked and fell back into Susanna's arms. She nearly toppled over from his weight tumbling into her. The rifle dropped and then Harry began to slide off the horse, Susanna desperately grabbing at him.

"No," she screamed.

The Lawyer fired at Creole and nailed him in the leg. Creole cried out, his horse turning senselessly from a hard tug of the reins where the injured man clutched at the fresh wound.

"Creole, he's wide open. Take your shot while you can, dammit!" Kimbrough yelled from the ground, his own horse had run off, abandoning him.

Three quick spurts splintered the charred wood all around him, but The Lawyer managed to duck down fast, no hits. He knew Kimbrough would have to reload. He popped up, ready to shoot. Kimbrough saw him and dropped his gun, took up another from a holster on his left hip. A new addition. Kimbrough ran to the tree stump where Ruth hid. He grabbed her and stood her up, putting the gun to her temple.

"Give yourself up, lawyer. It's you or her. You decide."

Kimbrough stood across the clearing, a good forty feet away. Ruth struggled in front of him, whipping her body back and forth across his. Impossible to get a shot in and not hit her. Thoughts of his wife flashed in his head. This was all for her. If he gave up now, her death would go unavenged. But, to sacrifice another innocent woman …

The gun trembled in his outstretched hand.

"What's it gonna be?" Kimbrough drew back the hammer on his gun.

"Dammit, he's mine." Creole circled his horse and came racing through the clearing, gun leading the way and aiming at The Lawyer.

A blast cut across the air from behind The Lawyer. Creole fell back and nearly flopped out of his saddle. The Lawyer turned to see Susanna with the Remington in her arms, tears running down and streaking through the ash caked on her face.

Creole half sat up with a scream in his throat. He charged his horse forward across the clearing toward Susanna. She stood with the Remington firm in her hands as Creole churned up a black cloud beneath him until his horse looked like a rider from the pages of Revelations. Susanna sighted down the barrel and fired when Creole was only six feet away. The shot knocked him from his saddle and he fell, dead before he hit the ground. The horse sped past her and Susanna spun, dropping the rifle as she was knocked to the ground beside Harry.

Seeing Susanna stand up against the outlaw, Ruth felt a surge within her. She let loose a scream and took Kimbrough's arm in her hands like a barbequed rib and bit down. Kimbrough howled and tried to wrench his arm away, but she was bit in like a wolverine.

Daylight swelled between them. The Lawyer fired. Kimbrough dropped his gun and clutched at his gut.

Ruth loosened her bite and let him fall away. The Lawyer fired again. Blooms of red were already spreading on his shirt. He landed face up in the ash, his eyes wide and his mouth moving in a silent scream.

Ruth ran. She moved quickly across the clearing and fell to her knees at Susanna's side.

The Lawyer walked slowly to where Kimbrough lay, his gun at the ready the whole time. He stood over Kimbrough and watched him gasp for air.

"For my wife," he said. Kimbrough's pupils went black with fear as a bullet went through his head.

CHAPTER SEVENTEEN

Susanna held Harry, telling him over and over how much she loved him and that he'd be okay.

"His breathing is strong," Ruth said to The Lawyer as he approached. "I think he'll be fine."

"I'm glad to hear it," he replied, genuinely relieved.

"Your face," she said. She wiped a hand across his cheek and it came back black.

He clapped at his pants, letting loose clouds of ash. "Just a bit of soot. Are you okay?"

"I'm alright, thanks to you."

"Don't thank me," he said. "I was the one who brought this to your door."

"No. I was the one who brought *you* to my door. What happened after that nobody could predict."

They began brushing off as best they could when they heard the clatter of a wagon coming near. The replacement appeared with the livery boy driving.

At the sight of Harry lying on the ground, the boy jumped down to help The Lawyer and Ruth load him into the wagon, Susanna remaining next to her intended's side.

"See he gets to the doctor straightaway." The Lawyer took out a few coins from his money pouch, and handed it to the boy who nodded and turned to leave.

As they watched the wagon dash away, Ruth said to The Lawyer with a faint smile, "Suzy won't be coming back to this valley."

The Lawyer placed a hand on her shoulder for he knew what alone felt like. "I'll round up the horses, and we'll head back to the ranch together."

* * *

The house was ruined on one side. The chimney had collapsed, the wall caved in. Fire hadn't taken the whole building, but that was about the best they could say about it. The bedrooms were intact as well as the barn. Belle's body was gone, and they presumed the undertaker had already come by using the other trail.

Ruth went first taking a cold bath to wash off the soot. The Lawyer stayed far away from the barn where she bathed, picking up chimney bricks and stacking what he could salvage from the kitchen, busy work to keep an appropriate distance in the way of modesty.

Ruth treaded the same awkward dance while he cleaned up. After he had dressed, The Lawyer made a list of items she would need and volunteered to go into town for her.

She handed him his hat.

The Lawyer smiled as he turned it over in his hands, examining the bullet holes.

"I picked it up when we got you," Ruth said. "I wasn't sure we should. Silly thing, that hat."

"Thanks. It has sentimental value."

"It must. No other reason a man would keep it." She watched him perch it on his head. "I could sew up those holes for you."

"No, thanks, ma'am. That's something I need to remember."

He tipped the stovepipe and rode to town.

* * *

After he paid the undertaker and got the details for Belle's service, he checked in on Harry and Susanna at Doctor Reed's. Ruth would want to know everything when he returned.

"He's young and resilient, Mr. Smith. He'll be fine," the doc reassured.

"I'm thankful for that," The Lawyer said.

"Oh, Mr. Smith," Susanna nearly wept as she spoke, "we can't thank you enough."

"Ruth already tried. It's me who needs to thank you for finding and caring for me. I'd be just another snake bite case if you ladies hadn't."

Dr. Reed motioned to The Lawyer's leg. "Long as you're here, let me take a look at that."

The doctor applied a new salve and dressed it with a fresh bandage, then checked the wound on his head. "All's healing well … Belle did a fine sewing job."

The Lawyer shook Harry's hand. "I'm in your debt, son."

"If it wasn't for all this, I might not have had the courage to finally ask Suzy to marry me. For that I'm in *your* debt."

"Well, treat her like gold, and we'll call it even."

"I'll do that, sir."

The Lawyer hugged Susanna and left.

* * *

Before heading back to the ranch, he stopped by the Western Union office. He sent off a cable many miles away to a man he hadn't seen in months. A man with information.

He ate a hearty meal while waiting and took the opportunity to get a shave and a haircut. When he was finished he asked to borrow one of the barber's brushes and he gave his hat a good dusting.

By the time he got back to Western Union, a reply was there for him. He read it once, nodded to himself, and tucked the note away in his chest pocket.

* * *

Back at Ruth's he delivered some essentials, told her the rest were coming by wagon, along with some help to rebuild.

"Not that you need it," he added.

"I had a glimmer of hope that you'd stick around."

"Afraid I can't." There never seemed to be any romance in it, from what he could tell. Seeing Ruth's eyes right then, he wasn't so sure. After what they'd been through, it would be understandable for feelings to develop. But his mind was already on the trail ahead.

"You have more men to kill, don't you?"

The Lawyer looked to the horizon, then met her gaze. "One."

"And then it'll be finished?"

"I don't know that it'll ever be finished. Not after what I've seen and done. Maybe the trail I'm on only goes one way."

"Are you going far?"

"Place called Freeville, New York."

"New York is a week's travel from here."

"I suppose it is."

Ruth put her hands over his, looked at him with the wet shine of tears in her eyes.

"I hope you find peace, Mr. Smith."

"My name … it's Justus Miller. And if I do find peace, Miss Ruth, I'm willing to bet it looks like this valley."

ABOUT THE AUTHOR

 Eric Beetner is a writer and TV editor living in Los Angeles where he hosts the Noir at the Bar series. He's been voted Most Criminally Underrated Author (Stalker Awards) one of the 10 Best Writers You've Never Heard Of (Dead End Follies) and the subject of a Why The F*ck Aren't You Reading? column in LitReactor. Author of more than a dozen novels and over 70 published short stories he constantly wonders why nobody has heard of him. Right now he is probably in his office, typing.

Also by Eric Beetner

Rumrunners
The Year I Died Seven Times
Nine Toes In The Grave
The Devil Doesn't Want Me
Criminal Economics
Dig Two Graves
White Hot Pistol
Stripper Pole At The End Of The
  World
A Bouquet Of Bullets: Stories
Fightcard: Split Decision
Fightcard: A Mouth Full Of Blood

with JB Kohl:
One Too Many Blows To The
  Head
Borrowed Trouble
Over Their Heads

with Frank Zafiro:
The Backlist
The Short List

THE YEAR I DIED SEVEN TIMES — Deaths = 7   Body count = 1

Well, okay, there were more bodies than that once the year was over. But for me, I wasn't going to let a little thing like death stop me from finding out what happened to the girl of my dreams.

* * * * *

In this one-of-a-kind novel, amateur investigator Ridley tests the limits of what a man will go through for true love. With the help of trained assassins and a stoner best friend, Ridley is thrown head-first into a dark world of drugs, kidnapping and violence. As a detective, he's not the best. Not even close. But Ridley is determined to find his girl — or die trying.

"... another excellent title from Beetner"   **—Dan Malmon**
Crimespree Magazine

"A fast paced story with enough twists and turns to keep the reader engaged until the end."   **—Brian Lindenmuth**
Editor for *Spinetingler Magazine*
and Snubnose Press

More in the Edward A. Grainger series
THE LAWYER

SIX GUNS AT SUNDOWN   ERIC BEETNER

Big Jim Kimbrough, left tracks to the small town of Sundown, Arkansas, where The Lawyer learns his prey has already moved on. But he can't leave after he witnesses a black man named Josiah being dragged behind a horse, the man's only crime is allegedly taking food from a white man's table, and is about to be lynched.

THE RETRIBUTIONERS   WAYNE D. DUNDEE

When the town of Emmett, Texas, is marked by the Selkirk gang and the local marshal murdered, The Lawyer is asked by the town's influential residents to track down the reprehensible outfit. But he has little use for the narrow-minded bigots that won't stand behind the remaining deputy—a black man named Ernest Tell.

STAY OF EXECUTION   WAYNE D. DUNDEE

One horrific, soul-scarring day J.D. Miller returned home to find his entire family slaughtered—the charred remains scarcely recognizable in the smoldering ruins of what had once been their house. Like a phoenix rising out of the ashes, The Lawyer—a killing machine—was born, and he's leaving a blood-splattered revenge trail as he searches out the men who murdered his family.

www.beattoapulp.com